The
BALTIMORE
BOOKIES

BY

Leonora "Peachy" Dixon

Printed in the United States of America
Book design by Denise McDonald

First printing, 2020

ISBN 978-0-578-64300-7

Rose Garden Press
3510 Claremont Street
Baltimore, MD 21224

The
BALTIMORE
BOOKIES

A Story of Greed and Misconception

To Mr & Mrs Howard Carden.
Thank you for everything
that you do for me

By

Leonora "Peachy" Dixon

Best Wishes
Love
Peachy

10/9/21

ACKNOWLEDGEMENTS

I would like to thank Ms. Diane Carliner for the wonderful article she wrote about me. Also my daughter Anna Maria Carpenter who helped me with my book. I would also like to thank Karli Murray for the many times she came to help me as well. Also my cousin Ronald *Di Pietro* who introduced me to Mr. Raymond McAlwee who helped me publish and get my books out there, Denise McDonald for designing my books, Fr. Bob Albright, Sr. Patricia Nightingale, and Barbara Ellen Thomas for the many times they helped me with my book.

Finally, I am forever thankful for my brother Vincent DiPietro's help throughout the years,

PROLOGUE

Kathy's city is a vibrant one, full of excitement and many thriving businesses. People coming to Baltimore always want to visit the Inner Harbor and our beautiful National Aquarium.

The Aquarium was constructed in Baltimore by the efforts of our fabulous mayor at the time, William Donald Schaefer. Visitors at the Inner Harbor and the Aquarium have the opportunity to visit the many different restaurants and specialty shops located there.

Downtown Baltimore has many thriving companies. One of the businesses is The Venable LLP which has grown into an American Lawycr Global firm. The firm is located at 750 East Pratt Street, Suite 900. They have more than 800 professionals who represent clients in multi-billion dollar transactions, complex commercial litigation matters, Maryland corporate matters, and local government issues. The firm spends countless hours of pro bono representation for needy individuals through the region.

Many residents and visitors shop at The Joseph A. Banks Company. It has been in business since 1905. It is located at 100 East Pratt Street near the Inner Harbor. This business accommodates men with business attire who work in the many businesses located downtown. George Ghartey is the manager in this store.

They provide services for all of the visitors who come to our great and beautiful City.

Another company is the *Baltimore Business Journal* located at 36A Charles Street in Suite 2500. It is a multi-media company covering local business and breaking news. It gives its customers a competitive edge of what is happening in our town and also nationally. It helps businesses make their many difficult decisions for their businesses.

Many have attended events in the Convention Center. It is the host to many different businesses that come to our City. The center constantly holds many different events there. They have the Boat show, the Car show, the Fireman's convention, and the Comic-Con group convention to name just a few. The people from the Gardening and Supply businesses come to the Convention Center for their conventions also.

Many local people display their wares in and around the downtown area. Some display their goods out of their vehicles on the streets of Baltimore. One of those people who did this was a young man named Kevin Scott. He got his inspiration and enthusiasm from his Mother who owned and operated her own restaurant in Baltimore. He bought suits and shirts and went downtown in his Chevy pickup truck. He dressed in style every day always wearing the best clothes. Kevin sold his shirts and suits to many lawyers that had their offices downtown. After he became more popular he moved his business to a building near the Park Sausage building on Belair Road. As he got stronger he remodeled the building and sold men's clothes there. His business grew.

As you pass the Inner Harbor with all its glamour, you come to an area that is known as Little Italy. One of the reasons this area is called this is because when the ships landed in the Harbor years ago, people who came off of the boats were of Italian descent. They didn't travel far and they made their homes in this section of town that is now known as Little Italy.

The men were experienced brick layers and because of this they were the people who were contracted to build many of the buildings that are located in the downtown area of Baltimore. As you drive downtown you can see the great details on the buildings. They were constructed by many of the men who came to Baltimore from Italy.

Some of the men were farmers. They created small farms near their homes. They grew vegetables for their families to eat. The women used the vegetables that their husbands grew to make meals for their families. The women were naturally born wonderful cooks. Because of their fabulous cooking skills some of the women opened little restaurants in the area. After they opened their businesses, most of the women were able to make a good living.

Other women who arrived from Italy went to work in the clothing industry. They were great seamstresses because they made clothes for their families while they lived in Italy.

Kathy's family is of Italian descent, and they were farmers, bakers and seamstresses. Her father's family came from Abruzzi. Her father's mother's name was Annarella and her grandfather's name was Gaetano. They were both from Abruzzi. They were married in 1901 and came to America in 1905.

They already had three children when the family made the ocean crossing to America. Kathy's grandmother Annarella was pregnant with her father, Carmen. The trip to America was not a pleasant one for her. She was terribly sick the entire time she was coming to America.

Her third child Dominic (Mimi) was very small at this time. A fourteen-year-old Italian boy named Bernardino DiPasquale watched him on the boat from Italy to America for Kathy's grandmother. Along with other family members, her grandfather Gaetano made his living by owning and operating a bakery in East Baltimore. They sold bread on a horse and buggy to all the neighbors who lived in East Baltimore.

Kathy's mother's family came from Naples. They came to America in1914. Her grandmother lived in Naples in the region of Atripalda in southern Italy. Their home was on top of a hill that overlooked the clear water of the Tyrrhenian Sea. The family owned and operated an extraordinary vineyard there. People from all over Italy journeyed to their vineyard to buy grapes to make their wine.

Her grandfather Raphael was a lawyer while in Italy and he was very well respected by everyone there. However, he could not acquire a license to be a lawyer in America, resulting in him not being able to practice law here in America. People knew he was an intelligent person though. They would come to him for advice all the time. He helped many people with all of their many problems. These people that he helped were not familiar with the American customs.

Since Raphael couldn't be a lawyer here he acquired a job working for the Metropolitan Life Insurance Company. At first, people thought he was using the money they gave him for his own purposes. They did not understand what life insurance was about until after one of his clients passed away. When Kathy's grandfather paid the family the insurance money, the people understood what having insurance meant. People then began to trust him.

There was another family, the Guerriero family, who immigrated to the United States from Sicily. After moving to many states in America the family finally settled in Baltimore in 1932. The Guerriero family opened a grocery store on Chester Street in Baltimore. Their son John worked in the grocery store with them. While he worked in the store, it became John's passion.

As soon as he returned from the war John received his father's blessing to take over the family grocery store. John worked hard and eventually he turned the grocery store into a wholesale food distribution business. He moved the company to Little Italy. He named it Continental Foods which he owned for over fifty years. While growing his business, John met a wonderful woman named Angeline Fedeli in a market in Little Italy. After dating Angie for a while they married in 1955.

John, or as he loved to be called, Giovanni, and his wife Angie, had a daughter. Her name was Diana, but he used to call her his "little flower." Diana met her future husband Rick and they fell in love and were married. As their family grew, Diana and Rick gave Angie and Giovanni many grandchildren. Giovanni's family was the center of his universe. Giovanni was known as a hard worker and generous individual with a dynamic, humorous, and compassionate personality.

As you pass Little Italy, you come to the area known as Fells Point. This is the section of town where many ships docked. Sailors frequented the many bars in the area when they docked there. Fells Point has cobblestone streets which have been there forever. One of the bars in Fells Point happened to be the last bar that Edgar Allen Poe visited before he passed away. It is called

"The Horse you came in on." Today, besides all the bars in Fells Point there are also many second hand shops, specialty shops, and restaurants. This area is frequented by many tourists, day and night. Young people go there on the weekends to celebrate with their friends.

※

Another company located in Fells Point was formed in Baltimore in 1974. It is called TBC, Inc. The company is an advertising agency. They promote public relations in the U S of A. This Company also provides broadcasting and film production for companies in Baltimore and beyond. They provide direct marketing for sports, entertainment marketing, strategic planning, traditional media, and unconventional media services. The TBC Inc. has been in business for forty-five years. The company is now located in the Natty Boh building.

※

As soon as you pass Fells Point you come to the area known as Canton. It is also located near the water. Back in the day, when sailors landed in Canton, they frequented the bars that were located in this area. It is a thriving area in our town where young professionals reside today.

When young people moved into Canton, they started to improve the area by remodeling their homes. They transformed this area into a beautiful section of Baltimore. There are also restaurants and little shops located in the Canton area. In the evening the people who live there can go out to eat and have a night on the town.

Another individual who owned and operated a restaurant in Canton, was Scunny. He opened "Nacho Mamas" in 1994 and he opened "Mama's on the Half Shell" in 2004. He had a promising future and was always trying to improve Baltimore.

Scunny got involved with the Natty Boh beer company. Natty Boh beer used to be made right here in Baltimore. Scunny wanted to bring it back to life. He promoted the beer in his business. He wanted to bring back the beer to Baltimore that our fathers and grandfathers used to drink. My father used to drink Natty Boh beer also and his nick name was Boh. I became intrigued and wanted to find more about Patrick Scunny McCusher.

Scunny, as all of his friends would call him, was a very generous person. He loved Baltimore. He would give you the shirt on his back. Scunny did the same thing to Canton that Mayor Schafer did for Baltimore. He was a one of a kind person.

Scunny was a big advocate for the children who had cancer. Saint Casimir's church would house the children and their parents in one of their properties in Canton. While the children were there, Scunny donated meals to the children. He also provided meals for the children during Thanksgiving and Christmas.

Another business in Canton on the square is called Gladdagh's Pub. It is owned and operated by Vivian, along with her son Michael. Vivian told her a little history about how her and her son's business came about.

Vivian's Mom and Dad, Eva and Dominic Speca, owned a business in Highlandtown in the 1960's. Named Speca's Lounge, it was located on the corners of Conkling and Pratt Streets. Their business was always busy. All of their food was homemade. They even served crabs. Many neighborhood people frequented their business. Their neighbors loved their food and they could also meet some of their neighbors there. It turned into a huge neighborhood gathering place.

As time went on, Vivian's father, Dominic, found out there was a business available downtown on Chase and Biddle Streets. The business had an Irish theme. It was called Denny & Joey's Irish pub. Dominic took over this new business. Because it had an Irish theme, Dominic put a tent outside on Saint Patrick's Day. When he did this, there would be a huge party there on Saint Patrick's Day. Dominic owned this business in the 1970's until the 1980's. This was the start of the Irish theme in Vivian's Italian family.

Vivian's son, Michael, was a liquor salesman. In 1995, Michael told his mother that there was a pub available on the square in Canton. The business was called Ed's Lounge. It was located at 2918 O'Donnell Street. It was only one building. It had no kitchen and not too much of anything else.

Michael explained to his mother how the neighborhood of Canton was growing. Vivian, who lived nearby, started checking the area out and she liked what she was seeing. She envisioned what the business could become.

Vivian and Michael opened the Pub in the spring of 1995. They have owned and operated the pub for twenty four years. Vivian and Michael are very congenial people. They are always at their business to greet and mingle with their customers.

There is a town in Ireland called Galway. It's symbol stands for Friendship, Loyalty, and Love. This is how the name for the business Gladdagh's Pub began.

Because Vivian's father put a tent outside his business on Saint Patrick's Day, Vivian decided to do the same thing to her business. There is a huge tent outside Gladdagh's Pub on Saint Patrick's Day. There is a band in the tent that plays music there the whole day during the Saint Patrick Day celebration.

Inside the pub is a sign reading "Cead -Mile-Failte." The sign means 100,000 hundred thousand hugs.

After they owned the business for several years, they expanded to 2916 and 2914. They have owned the business for twenty four years.

Vivian gives to many charities. One of her favorite charities is the Wounded Warriors. Her all time favorite charity is for the children that go to the Saint Jude's Hospital. Vivian contributes a great deal to the Saint Jude's Hospital charity. Cead, Mile, Failte. – The Clarke Family.

❋

Now you come to the section of town known as Highlandtown or East Baltimore. Kathy has lived in this area for over forty years. Construction is going on all through her neighborhood. There are young professionals moving into the area, making a huge difference to this section of town. People talk to one another once again. Neighbors look out for each other, and it is beautiful. What a wonderful thing to happen to this neighborhood after forty years. It is finally coming back to life!

Highlandtown has a grocery business called Di Pasquale's. Luigi Di Pasquale was the original owner of Di Pasquale's grocery store. This business started in 1914 on Claremont and Dean Street by Luigi Di Pasquale, Sr. One of Luigi's sons, Mr. Lou Di Pasquale, ran the business for several years at this location. Lou was born in America but his father Luigi was born in Abruzzi, Italy. This was the same town Kathy's grandparents Di Pietro's were from.

All of the Luigi Di Pasquale children were born upstairs from the business in Highlandtown. When Luigi Di Pasquale Sr. became sick in 1958, Lou Di Pasquale, Jr. was called by his mother. She asked him to help in their local business in Highlandtown. Luigi passed away in 1959 which left Lou Jr. to run the business.

Lou Jr. operated his father's business for several years. After being at the same location for several years Lou's children moved their business to a larger location. This location was one street from their father's location on Gough and Dean Streets in 1988. It gave them more room to store the supplies they sold in the store. They also ran a wholesale business. Joseph and Sabrina, along with Joseph's two sisters, Anna Maria and Angel, run the business today.

The Di Pasquale's business has been interviewed by Guy Fieri from Diners, Drive-Ins and Dives several times. These interviews have helped Di Pasquales become very popular. People from as far of Washington, D.C. and Virginia frequent their business. The food that is served at Di Pasquales is all homemade. They make homemade pasta, sauce, mozzarella balls, rice balls, Lasagna noodles, and Lasagna. They also make homemade meat balls and soups. Recently the Di Pasquales have celebrated being in business for 100 years.

✿

Another successful business in Highlandtown was owned and operated by Augie Ruggerio. He opened his shop in the 1930's. Later, Augie's son Michael started working in his father's shop. His sister, Lucy, took care of the books for him. Augie's grandson, David, came to help his grandfather out. He missed his grandfather and he wanted to be close to him. The only way he knew how to do this was to go to his grandfather's shop. He was thirteen years old when he did this. David closed his grandfather's shop in 2016. He has taken over many businesses in this area and restored them to the luster that they are today. David's main office is located at 126 N. Clinton Street. David's wife, Shelly, works there and takes care of the paperwork for him.

David, a very progressive businessman, was always looking for other sites in Highlandtown. He found an old dilapidated building on Haven and Baltimore Streets. David bought this quarter-million square foot property on eight acres from the Metro Development Company nine years ago. This location is where the trains used to deliver goods to companies in Baltimore. It was dormant for thirty years. Even though David has turned this area into an amazing site, he kept the facade of a boiler in one of his properties. He needed a crane to put it there. There are 150 companies located there today. Among this collaborate of businesses there is a restaurant called the Boiler Room Restaurant.

You will also find a brewing company that manufactures beer right on the premises located there today. They only sell the beer that is made on site. During the summer months they show movies there. David kept his properties very professional. He takes pride in his business. This is one of the most amazing properties located in Highlandtown today.

As the lives of the good people in Baltimore enfold, you will soon see a path of destruction created by one person. Acts of violence that have been committed to the people of East Baltimore will impact their lives forever.

CHAPTER ONE
The Rude Awakening

The wonderful city of Baltimore, consisting of happy families and thriving businesses, soon becomes one of shock and disbelief. The effects of what happens to the people of East Baltimore would last in the minds of all the people who live there.

While coming home from working the night shift one evening, Kathy noticed people hanging around on the corner past her home. She thought to herself, how odd it was for people to be hanging around the corner during this time of night. After all of the marvelous improvements to this neighborhood, there are people who are trying to degrade the neighborhood. They hang out on corners and cause disruption to businesses and residents of Highlandtown.

The next morning, Kathy saw a news flash on TV. A young woman was found badly beaten in East Baltimore, right down the street from my home. How someone could hurt an innocent woman for no reason at all is unbelievable. Detectives immediately began their investigation of the situation. They discover a ring of destruction and gambling in this wonderful City of ours right here in East Baltimore.

Milton, a local resident, is also Kathy's friendly mailman. He has a medium build, with sandy colored hair and brown eyes. He has the warmest smile. When he smiles, he makes you want to smile with him. Milton is a rather handsome person. His average

build and height, without being overweight is probably due to all the hours he walks working as a mailman. He always looks out for all the neighbors. He knows most of them by their names. He often stops and talks to the neighbors if they are outside while he is delivering their mail. Most of the people he delivers mail to like him a lot. They all want to talk to Milton, because he always has something funny to tell them.

Most of the homes had porches in front. Milton had to climb the steps of the porch-front homes to deliver mail. During the summer months the people who live in the porch-front homes would sit on their porches and watch the children playing in the school lot ball field across the street from their homes.

Most of the people who lived in these homes had them re-modeled. The people of East Baltimore took their homes back to the splendor they had when they were built years ago. They had their floors remodeled by the Elias Wilf Corporation.

The Elias Wilf Corporation began in 1915 by Elias Wilf.

Elias started his company by selling oilcloth and linoleum to his customers. Some of the older people who lived in Highlandtown knew Mr. Wilf because he lived near them. Their confidence in Mr. Wilf was the reason they called Mr. Wilf to remodel their floors. He was a competitor in his field and he took great care to the families he serviced. Today, the grandson of Mr. Wilf, Mr. Arnold Cohen has taken over the business for his grandfather. Mr. Cohen is the reason the company has expanded into the largest carpet and flooring business in the country today. This company helped the people from East Baltimore bring their homes back to the splendor they were meant to be when they were built years ago.

As Milton got closer to the homes that were across the street from the school lot, he could see there was something or someone lying there. Because it was overcast on this day it was difficult for Milton to make out what was there. He kept walking closer to get a better view. That's when he found out it was a woman lying on the ground. Milton could see the woman was young. She appeared to be in her twenties. He could tell she was badly beaten. The woman's head was bleeding severely on the side where her assailant hit her. He leaned over the woman to see if he could do something to help the woman out. When Milton saw the severity of her injuries, he realized he couldn't do anything to help her. He knew she needed medical attention, so he called the police and an ambulance.

The school lot where the woman was found is huge. The front of the school lot is the school where the children in the neighborhood attended. The back of the school lot opens up into the play area. It had different activities for the school children to play. The school lot has a playground, baseball, and soccer field. The end of the school lot was surrounded by businesses that had been located there for many years. The school lot was a secluded area in the evening with hardly any lighting. This would contribute to the reason why no one could see anything.

Later when the police responded to the call, they surrounded the area. The police started putting yellow crime tape all around the playground, so no one could enter it while they were doing their investigating. Finally, the ambulance arrived to help the woman and take her to the hospital.

You could not drive anywhere in the area because the police had the area all blocked off. When it was time for the children to go to recess, they were not allowed to go outside this day. The police shut the whole area of Highlandtown down. This was the first time anything happened like this in the area. All the neighbors were very upset. On this morning though, the whole neighborhood woke up to see what was going on. Soon the street was full of many older people who lived there. They knew that today would be different for the neighbors than all the rest. Their whole neighborhood was shaken because of this horrible incident that happened in their area.

The TV reporters were giving as many details as they knew on the air. Ron Matz and Richard Scher from Channel 13 were questioning Captain Dave of the police. He was trying to answer the many questions Ron and Richard were putting to him. On TV all the other news had stopped to bring the Baltimore public all the details of what was going on at the crime scene. Many other reporters from the different TV stations came to Highlandtown to question the people from the neighborhood.

David Collins from Channel 11 was also in the neighborhood questioning the people to find out if they had seen anything. Mary McKenzie from Fox 45 came to the streets of Highlandtown. Mary was interviewing the neighbors, asking them if they heard or saw anything. Jamie Costello from Channel 2 was circulating his way through Highlandtown asking the neighbors questions about this unfortunate incident.

The neighborhood of Highlandtown consisted of all working class people. People who live in the neighborhood do what they have to do to survive every day. There are only two very wealthy people who live in the neighborhood. These people are very private about their lives. There are only a very few people who know of their wealth. They are the people who work at the Old Line Bank in the area. These wealthy people live a very modest life style. They had invested in the stock market in the early years. They bought Intel and Apple early. This is why they are well off today.

The police questioned some of the residents that had been gathering outside. Most of the people who lived across from the school lot were retired people. They told the police that they went to bed early, sometimes as early as nine or ten o'clock. They told the police no one ever heard or saw anything. The police found out that one of the residents worked the night shift. He was a middle-aged man with dark brown hair and hazel eyes. The man's name was Angelo. He had the start of a beard because he hadn't shaved yet. He was a little on the heavy side.

CHAPTER TWO
The Investigation

When the police questioned Angelo, he told them he came home around one o'clock in the morning. He told them that he did not notice anything strange in the school lot during this time. He said that he had just gotten off of work and he was tired. He wasn't paying attention to the rest of his neighborhood at this time. He told the police that he had one thing on his mind and that was sleep. He told the police he drank a beer and then he watched a little TV. Since there wasn't anything interesting on the TV, he went to bed. Highlandtown was such a safe residential area where many families lived. Over the months that followed many people were questioned and leads were checked out that took the police nowhere.

As a result of the police being called, the captain of the police called in his two best detectives to work on the case. The two detectives assigned to the investigation were Ed Deluca and Rosie Ramirez. These two detectives have been working together ever since they entered the police academy many years ago. They worked hand and hand together on the streets of Baltimore. They were very thorough when they investigated crimes. This is the reason why Captain Dave assigned them to the case.

Deluca and Ramirez started surveying the neighborhood, asking the people who lived there if anyone heard or had seen anything strange the day before this happened. The neighbors told the detectives they never noticed anything that wasn't normal in the neighborhood. Later, the two detectives talked to Angelo who didn't give them any more information. Then they went to question Milton the mailman. Milton explained to the detectives the same things he told the police earlier. He told the detectives it appeared that the woman tried to fight the person off. They asked him how he knew this. Milton told the police the woman had bruises on her arms where it appeared to him that the woman tried to defend herself. The detectives asked Milton if he had noticed anyone who didn't belong in the neighborhood. Milton told the detectives that the neighborhood appeared to be the same as it had been every day that he delivered mail there.

The detectives were concerned that they never got any descriptions of strangers hanging around the area in the weeks before this incident happened. The neighbors told the police they just went about their daily routine with no expectations of anything bad that was going on in their neighborhood. When the detectives heard this, they realized there would be many more hours of investigation ahead of them. Even though the police combed the whole area they couldn't come up with any clues.

There were also many businesses in the area that had been located here for many years. There were restaurants, beauty shops, specialty shops, grocery stores, bakery stores, and barber shops. The people who owned these shops were upset, because they didn't want anything to happen in their neighborhood. They depended on the neighbors who lived in the area. They needed the business from these people to sustain their business to help them pay their bills.

Ron Matz and Richard Scher from Channel 13 stayed in the area because they knew there might be something for them to find out. They need to tell the TV audience something. When they couldn't get any answers from Captain Dave, Ron and

Richard decided to start to question the neighbors. While conducting their investigating the reporters found out that there are two very wealthy people who live in the neighborhood. The reporters also found out that the woman who was hurt was related to the rich people.

As soon as the reporters found this out, they believed they had something to go on. They asked the neighbors where the rich people lived. At first the neighbors were reluctant to give the reporters any information about these people. When the neighbors wouldn't give the reporters this information, this made the reporters believe that this investigation might lead to something big.

Richard Scher and Ron Matz went back to the TV station. They started to look up information on this area of East Baltimore. After they delved more into the past history of this area, they came up with something important. The information they found out was very interesting. The people who worked in these areas years ago were hard working individuals. Although the men worked hard during the years to take care of their families, some found an easier way to make money.

Ron and Richard found out that people from Vegas came to Baltimore to talk to the Italian people to get them involved in the numbers racket. People from Vegas told the people from Baltimore that they could keep their jobs. The Vegas people told the Italian people if they took book for them then they could make more money to take care of their families.

As a result of many years of hard labor, many of the residents from Little Italy and East Baltimore jumped at an opportunity that could make some extra money. All they had to do was take bets from people on numbers that came out every day. They also had to take bets on the different games that were being played in America. The Vegas people showed the Italians how easy it would be for them to make some extra money. When the Vegas people finally convinced the Italian people of their plan, a huge gambling operation started here in the City. People from different parts of Baltimore would come down to Little Italy and East Baltimore to place bets every day. These areas became a very popular place for people from the different sections of town to visit.

When Ron and Richard came back to East Baltimore they asked the neighbors why they thought this woman was being singled out. The people wanted to be on TV so they were anxious to talk to the reporters. The people told the reporters that maybe she was beaten because it had something to do with the rich people who lived there. After Ron and Richard heard this they wanted to find out where the rich people lived. While questioning the neighbors they finally found out where the wealthy people lived.

Ron and Richard went to the rich people's home but when they got there the people would not talk to them. They told the reporters they had no comment and slammed the door. Ron and Richard decided that they would keep investigating the situation at a later date.

CHAPTER THREE
The Burlesque Club

In Kathy's neighborhood, there was a burlesque show bar. The shows that were performed there were real class acts. They were not like other strip places. The women who worked at the strip show bar in East Baltimore gave the illusion that they were going to strip. The women who performed there never really stripped all the way. They would take a glove off and toss it to the crowd. Then they would take a stocking off and flip it into the crowd. When they did this, the men would go crazy wanting to see more. This is why the burlesque club was always busy.

The women who performed kept the men returning with the illusion that one time the women may reveal more of themselves. Of course they never did, but the anticipation that they might do this kept the place busy all the time. Most of the women who worked there were single and had children. They had to work to support their children. This was the one place the women could work to make some great money to support their children and themselves.

Some of the women who worked at the club lived in the neighborhood. They frequented the many shops in the area. They became friends with the people who owned the businesses, because they shopped in their stores.

One of the shops the strippers frequented was the local beauty shop. Most of the girls who worked at the strip club had their hair fixed every week. In order to entice the men to come back to the club, the women wanted to look their best for the show they put on. The women needed the men to come back to the club over and over again. This enabled them to keep their jobs so they could support their children.

Two of the ladies who worked at the beauty shop were Phyllis and Clara. They became friends with the strippers, because they were their repeat customers. Phyllis was the original owner of the shop. She was a middle aged woman and had a medium height and a medium build. She had brown hair and blue eyes. She had owned the shop for many years. In fact, she lived upstairs from the shop. Her shop and her home were immaculate.

Clara was Phyllis' right hand girl. Clara worked many long hours there. She helped Phyllis tremendously in the shop. Clara was short with light brown hair and brown eyes. These two ladies and the rest of the beauticians who worked in the shop kept the beauty shop busy all the time.

The strippers would tell the beauticians stories of things that happened at the club. Then the beauticians and the strippers would laugh together at all the different ways the men behaved when they came into the club. The strippers also talked to the beauticians about their families. Some of the strippers came to the beauty shop twice a week to get their hair done. They were very conscious of the way they looked. They wanted to look good for their clientele.

There was a gay man who worked in the beauty shop. The man's name was Gene. All the girls had such a good time when they came to the shop because of Gene. They laughed with him all the time. He could relate to the strippers because they were both interested in the same thing. They all wanted to look good. He gave them tips on how to dress and how to wear their clothes. He told them if they dressed the way he told them it would make them more appealing to the men. The ideas Gene gave the women would keep the men more interested in them.

Of course the way Gene would describe things to the strippers, they would be so hilarious that he had everybody in the shop laughing all the time. He was a natural comedian. He played tricks on some of the customers. While they were under the dryer some of the customers would fall asleep. He had all kind of toys he would put on the customers while they were sleeping. When they woke up and saw what he did to them they would be upset for a little while. Because of all the funny antics he did he would have the customers constantly laughing. This was another reason the beauty shop was always busy.

After a couple of weeks passed, the beauticians realized that one of the strippers was not coming in for her appointments. The beauticians asked the police the name of the woman who was hurt down the street from their shop. This is how the beauticians found out the woman that had missed several of her appointments was the person who was injured in the school lot. The women's name was Nancy.

The beauticians started talking among themselves and they decided to start to collect money for their friend. They couldn't understand who would want to hurt such a nice person the way she was hurt. When the beauticians had the idea to collect money for the stripper, the other strippers started to collect money for their friend Nancy also. Everyone was concerned after this incident and the neighbors all wanted to help the woman out. The strippers told the beauticians that their business had slowed down.

As soon as the beauticians told the police that they knew the woman who was injured in the school lot, the police told the detectives. The detectives came to the beauty shop and started to ask the beauticians about the injured woman. The other strippers who came to the beauty shop told the detectives the person who was injured was a nice person. They told the detectives the woman had two children. The children are the reason why their friend Nancy worked there so she would be able to support them. Now they all wondered what would happen to the children. How were the children going to be able to take care of themselves since they were still very young?

The detectives, Deluca and Ramirez, wanted to know what her character was like. They wanted to know if she was mixed up with some shaky people or drugs. The beauticians told the detectives the woman was a clean, generous, very responsible, and wonderful person. They told the detectives she was just trying to make a living to support her children.

Then the strippers told the detectives about some weird people who were coming in the club. The information the strippers told the detectives gave them something to go on. After questioning the strippers, the detectives found out that the woman came from a very well respected family in the neighborhood.

Detectives Deluca & Ramirez went to all the other businesses in the area and started questioning the shop owners. The shop owners were very concerned about what had happened in their neighborhood. They couldn't afford to lose any business. They depended on the people who lived in the area to come into their shops. They didn't want anyone leaving the area because of what had happened in the neighborhood. They cooperated with the detectives and told them if they found out anything they would contact them.

While the detectives were questioning people in the neighborhood, they came upon a woman named Lucy. They hadn't interviewed her yet. Lucy was one of the local residents in the area. She was short with brown eyes and brown hair. After interviewing Lucy they found out some very good information.

She was working in her brother's car repair shop answering the phones and helping him with the paper work.

Lucy told the detectives she saw a strange looking man hanging around the neighborhood. Lucy said the man was tall and he had a weird look about him. She told the detectives she got bad vibes when he walked past her brother Michael's shop. Lucy described the man as tall and thin. She remembered this because Lucy was short. She said he had brown hair with a little gray running through it. She told the detectives that when he walked past her brother's shop she noticed he was walking with a limp.

At least this was something the detectives had to go on. The detectives thanked Lucy and told her they would get back to her. They also gave her their card and told her if she remembered anything else or saw the man again to please give them a call. This mystery had the police baffled, but after Lucy gave them some clues about the man it gave the detectives something to go on. They began looking for a tall person who walked with a limp.

The detectives went to see their captain. They told him they thought it would be a good idea if he would send some floaters to the burlesque bar. They told the captain to ask them to mingle with the customers and see if they could find something out. The detectives had somewhat of a description of the person they were looking for. After the detectives told Captain Dave this he agreed to send some floaters to the club to check the situation out. The captain believed they might be able to find something that would be important.

CHAPTER FOUR
The Second Disaster

As time passed, Kathy received a letter from the MVA informing her that she had to get her driver's license renewed. When she started to enter the MVA, or as it is better known today as the Motor Vehicle Administration, there was a heavy police presence. The police were directing traffic to one side of the parking lot. The MVA added a new wing in the 70s, and she thought this was the reason the police were directing traffic to that area.

The Administration has made many improvements to the MVA. They have enlarged the parking facilities to accommodate more people who come there for the various things that the Administration provides for the public. There is also a courtyard with many trees that were just planted recently to make the place look more attractive. They also added benches for the people to sit while they are waiting to get into the MVA. The place had no atmosphere until they added these features to it. In the back of this area is a small alcove. This is the area where they test the people who drive motorcycles.

There were long lines to enter the MVA on this particular day. Because of this Kathy started talking to the people who were waiting outside. She ran into a neighbor there. The Motor Vehicle Administration was so busy on the day they were both there. They sat and talked for a while about their families. They had known each other since they were children and both lived in the same neighborhood. The woman's name was Connie. She was short like Kathy with brown hair and brown eyes. They talked for about an hour. Because Kathy only had to renew her license, she was able to leave after she concluded her business. On the other hand, Connie had more business to take care of, so she had to stay longer.

While they were there they found out that recently someone had been beaten and left for dead on the premises. As the cleaning people went in the back to get the heavy cleaning apparatus to clean the building, they discovered the woman lying in the back of the building. This area has a lot of trailers located there. It is a secluded area. This same area is where the motorcycles are inspected.

The woman had been badly beaten and left there for dead. Who could do such an awful thing to a human being like this? The person who did this must have been a deranged individual. When the cleaning people found the woman they were very upset. They ran back into the building to inform people there what they had found.

Once again detectives Deluca and Ramirez were called in to investigate the situation. When they arrived at the scene they talked to the police who were examining what happened to the woman. They noticed the woman had been beaten exactly the same way as the other woman in East Baltimore was. Her perpetrator had struck her on the side of the head and she was bleeding profusely. It must have been a very sharp object for her to be bleeding this way. The detectives then began to question the people who worked at the MVA.

Deluca interviewed a woman who had worked at the MVA for years. Her name was Helen. She came to work early on this day to catch up on some paper work. Helen told Deluca she hadn't noticed anything strange until the cleaning people came in and told her what they found.

Helen was terribly upset because she was one of the first people to see the poor women in the condition that she was left in. Helen is a beautiful tall blonde lady with a slender build. She has a fabulous smile. When she smiles her eyes light up and she makes you want to smile with her. On this day, though, Helen was not smiling much, she was crying. The thought that someone could hurt another human being this way was unbelievable.

Helen told detective Deluca the woman must have fought her perpetrator off because she had bruises on her arms. Helen also told Deluca she noticed that some of her fingernails had been broken off. When Helen told Deluca this, he excused himself and went to call Captain David. Deluca told Captain David to get some of the forensic people to go to the hospital. Deluca told the Captain to tell the forensic people to get as much evidence from under the woman's fingernails as possible. Deluca told the captain the person he was interviewing told him that many of the woman's fingernails had been broken off. It appeared the woman tried to protect herself from her predator.

After Deluca called the captain, he went back to talk to Helen. He couldn't help but notice how beautiful Helen was. He made sure to get her phone number. He told Helen he needed to call her and question her further on what she had seen this morning. Even though he wanted to question her about the case he had other intentions. His intentions had to come later though because he had more important things to do today. Ed told Helen he would call her later during the day.

As soon as Deluca and Ramirez realized the similarities of the two cases they went back to East Baltimore to try to dig up more clues. As they interviewed people who lived in the neighborhood they discovered that the two women who were injured were related. They also found out that both of the women were related to some of the most prominent people who lived in East Baltimore. For the first time, while investigating these cases, they finally had a promising link. The detectives went to talk to these people.

The Del Judajea family lived in one of the biggest homes in East Baltimore. Their home was located on Bank Street which is a huge street in East Baltimore. Their home had a porch on the front of it and a balcony upstairs. The Del Judajea's home was located across the street from Hoehn's bakery. The bakery has been located in this area in Highlandtown for many years.

When Deluca and Ramirez entered the home of the Del Judajeas, they were very polite. The people were in their late sixties. They were Carmen and Philomena Del Judajea. They were well off because they worked hard in their early years. They also invested their money early in the stock market. This provided the income needed to live so well.

Carmen was a little on the heavy side, but not much. His hair was turning gray and he had brown eyes. His wife, Philomena stayed home every day. She was also short and a little on the heavy side. Her hair was turning gray and she had brown eyes. She spent her days cleaning and cooking for her husband. She wanted her home to be spotless. She cleaned everything in her home herself.

As the detectives entered their home they noticed how elaborate it was. The detectives told the Del Judajeas how nice their home was. Their furniture was all high end and very plush. Philomena had her living room furnished with huge solid oak chairs and sofa. The sofa and chair's fabric were covered with rich gold brocade. She wanted her furniture to be very sturdy. There were marble top end tables and a marble top coffee table that were imported from Italy. They also had marble lamps that also came from Italy.

All their furniture was purchased through the DeborahJohn Furnishings Company in Essex. Carmen knew John, the owner of the company very well and they were friends. John owned the furniture store along with his wife Deborah. This is why John named his store the DeborahJohn Furniture Store. The Del Judajeas always bought their furniture from John's company. John custom ordered the furniture for the Del Judajeas special all the time. Mr. John would make sure they would receive everything that they ordered on time.

There was a magnificent Persian rug under the coffee table. The rug was black with a beautiful flower design woven in it. They purchased the rug from the Next Day Floors Company because they knew the people who owned the rug company also. They became friends with all these different people that they met in a restaurant in Little Italy. The Del Judajeas have stayed friends with the Next Day Floor people for some time.

Their curtains were custom made by the people who worked at the JC Penny's store. The people would come into their homes and measure their windows to make sure they would fit just right. The fabric that Philomena picked was nylon because this fabric did not require much care. The people from JC Penny would come and install the curtains on the windows. Therefore Mrs. Del Judajea would not have to do anything to them.

As the detectives went further into their home they also noticed that they had all the latest technological equipment. There was a small alcove on the one side of their home that Carmen had all his computer equipment set up. Carmen purchased this equipment from the Staples store in East point.

There was a modern TV with all the equipment that went with their big screen TV. They purchased their TV from the Big Screen Store in Baltimore. They also met these people in their favorite restaurant in Little Italy.

Philomena invited the detectives into the kitchen for a cup of coffee. It was spotless, which Philomena made sure was clean every day. As the detectives went further into their home they told the Del Judajeas how sorry they felt for the things that were happening to their relatives. Mrs. Del Judajea had all the modern cooking equipment in her kitchen at her disposal. There was a huge Whirlpool refrigerator and a huge Thermador Pro Grand range. She needed all this modern day equipment so she would be able to prepare wonderful meals for her family.

When the detectives entered their kitchen they could see their yard in the back of their home. The Del Judajeas had several rose bushes located there. Rosie complimented Mrs. Philomena on her rose garden. Rosie told Philomena that roses take a lot of work and she could see they were well taken care of. The roses were very beautiful.

Mrs. Del Judajea fixed coffee for the detectives. The detectives wanted to make the Del Judajeas comfortable so when they started to ask them some questions, they wouldn't be nervous. The detectives didn't mention explicit things, they kept the conversation vague. They didn't insinuate that they thought the Del Judajeas had anything to do with the things that were happening to their relatives.

The detectives told the Del Judajeas they were both interested in the well-being of their relatives. The detectives told the Del Judajeas that it would be to their advantage if they could think of anyone who was doing this to their relatives. They made the Del Judajeas believe if they didn't talk to them, that something else might happen, even worse than already happened to them. They tried to make them believe that it was urgent for them to help them find the person or persons who are doing this to their relatives. The detectives wanted the Del Judajeas to help them with this case.

After the detectives questioned the Del Judajeas about the two women, they told the detectives that they had no idea why anyone would want to hurt their two relatives. They were actually related through marriage to these two women. The two women were married to their two nephews Giovanni and Vincenso. The Del Judajeas told the detectives they watched out for these women because their nephews used drugs. They told the detectives their nephews got involved with drugs and now they were hooked on them. Their nephews never contributed to helping their wives out with the children. The Del Judajeas helped the women out for this reason.

The detectives asked the Del Judajeas why they thought these two women were being singled out like this. The women who were beaten were poor working- class people. The Del Judajeas told the detectives that the women worked hard to support their children. The husbands of the women were their blood relatives. The women had nothing to give this person who was hurting them. They couldn't figure it out and this is what they told the two detectives.

The detectives wanted the Del Judajeas to believe that if they didn't talk to them about what was happening they might lose an opportunity to help them find the person who is doing this to their relatives. The detectives made them believe that it was urgent for them to help them find the person or persons who were doing this to their relatives. They wanted to make it personal and to the Del Judajea's advantage if they could help them with this case.

The detectives asked them to call them if they came across any more information. When the detectives could not get any more information from the Del Judajeas, they stood up to leave. The detectives wanted to see if they would ask them to stay and talk some more or if they were glad they were going to leave.

When the detectives could see that the Del Judajeas were ready for them to leave they said their goodbyes.

Later in the evening Deluca called Helen. He told her he would like to meet with her because he had more questions to ask her. But in reality he just used this as an excuse because he wanted to see her again. He asked her if they could meet somewhere in her neighborhood for coffee. He didn't want her to have to drive far. He told her he would come to her.

Deluca asked Helen if there was a Starbucks or Panera Bread near her home. He told her either one of those places would be a good place for them to meet and talk about the case. The meeting place they decided on was the Panera Bread. This place had a larger seating area and therefore they would be able to talk more privately. Deluca was getting excited about his meeting with Helen again.

Helen on the other hand just thought it was a meeting to talk about the case. She had no idea what Ed's intentions were. Even though she thought he was very nice she considered their meeting to be all about the investigation. On the other hand, she did think he was very handsome.

When they met, Deluca was trying to act all business-like, exactly the way he did when they met at the MVA. He kept asking her questions that pertained to the case, until eventually he started to ask her about her personal life. He asked her if she was married or dating anyone. He told her he didn't want to take up a lot of her time if she was involved with anyone. Helen told Deluca that she was not seeing anyone at the present time. She informed him that he didn't have to worry about him taking her away from someone else.

Of course, by now, Helen was getting curious about their chance meeting. Helen was also getting a little more interested in Deluca. He was very handsome and also very personal. He treated her with respect which was a great plus with her. They continued to talk and before they noticed it they had talked for over an hour.

Deluca finally told Helen he would like to take her out to dinner one evening. He was wondering if that would be okay with her. Helen was a little shy at first but then she told him she would like that very much. This was the start of the beginning of a new relationship for both of them.

CHAPTER FIVE
The Detectives

Rosie Ramirez and Ed Deluca have been partners for fifteen years. They knew each other's moves backwards and forwards. By now they knew each other's likes and dislikes. Ramirez was always the clean cut detective. She was the backbone that kept the two of them on track. She came to work every day in a nice clean outfit. She always wore jeans and a black jacket. Deluca sometimes wore the same outfit, but even though he was clean shaven and showered, at times his clothes left something to be desired.

They both entered the police force when they were young. They went to all the declassifying classes and all the grueling exercises required to join the police academy. After they passed all the tests they were accepted into the police department. Deluca and Ramirez spent many years together doing leg work for the other squads, specifically the domestic violent cases.

When they first joined the force Ed thought it was fun and exciting because it kept his adrenaline running. They both wanted to make this job a career. They thought it was a respectful profession to be in. They thought they could make a difference. Ed believed if he could help one person a year then he did his job.

The two detectives knew each other way back when they were regular cops. They worked hand and hand together for years on the streets of Baltimore. They helped each other through all the rough times that they experienced. Because of their hard times together, they actually became friends.

Rosie was also harassed when she entered the police department. The other police kept on her for sometime before Ed took up for her. It was Ed who stuck by her and was her friend through all the harassment she had to endure. Then and only then did the other police leave Rosie alone. Rosie was so grateful to have a partner who was also her friend on and off the squad.

Deluca gradually moved up to a different department. Then he was promoted to the department that investigates serious crimes. Soon Ramirez moved up to the serious crime unit also. Eventually they worked hand and hand on the most difficult cases. They worked so well together, and their thoroughness solved many crimes. Their hard work paid off in the end from all the many late nights that they had spent together investigating the crimes. They knew what the other one was thinking before they realized they knew it themselves. They always watched out for each other and because of this, they were great together.

When they first entered the police force as rookies, they thought being on the murder squad was the best thing ever. They looked up to the guys that were on this particular squad. They took all the harassments because they wanted to be on the homicide squad. They believed that they could solve many crimes. After they were finally able to get on the murder squad they realized it wasn't so great after all. All the murder squad consisted of was more long and gruesome hours of investigation after investigation.

Rosie is married to a wonderful man named Bernie. Bernie works for the *Baltimore Sun* Paper and that is how they met. Rosie was investigating a crime in the city when she met Bernie. He was the investigating reporter for the Baltimore Sun newspaper on the same case that Rosie was working on. So eventually, they were both kind of, sort of, working together.

Their work brought both of them together and they have been together ever since. They have been married for twelve years. They have two children, a boy and a girl. The boy is 8 years old and his name is Tyler. The girl is 6 and her name is Rachel.

Rosie and Bernie are still very much in love with one another. You can tell this because when they look into each other's eyes they still have the look of love.

Deluca, on the other hand, is a happy-go-lucky guy. He has been divorced for six years from his wonderful wife of fifteen years. Her name was Gracie. She could not stand the long hours of her husband being away from her because of his job. She also could not tolerate his heavy drinking. When he came home he would bring his job home with him. If he had a bad day, he kept talking about it to his wife over and over again. She wanted him to stop talking about it because he was home now. Gracie didn't understand why he kept talking about it. She didn't understand that the reason he did this was to get it out of his system. He wanted to relate to her the experiences that happened to him during the day, but she didn't want to hear it. Gracie wanted to have a conversation about something else. Gracie wanted him to hear about her day and tell him everything that happened to her. She wanted to tell him all the nice things that she did that day, but he wouldn't let her. He just kept talking about what happened to him. The arguments were getting worse and worse.

She was fed up with him bringing his work home with him. This was the reason for their constant bickering. Although this was a way for Ed to let go of his emotions, the fighting went on constantly between them. Soon Ed stayed at the bar a little longer. When he came home Gracie would be asleep and there would not be any confrontation.

Ed was also taking his frustrations out on Gracie, especially if something went wrong with his day. After many years of this behavior, Gracie couldn't take it any longer. She finally had enough. This was the main reason for their split and eventually led to their divorce.

This left Deluca a little lonelier and less caring about his appearance after their split. He let things go about himself. His appearance became somewhat less desirable.

Since Deluca's separation from his lovely wife Gracie of fifteen years, Ramirez has been Deluca's crutch. Ramirez was his friend for many years. She spent many evenings taking Deluca home after he had too much to drink. She even made sure he was in safe for the evening.

While they were working a case for many long hours together, she would always take care of him. They are very good together and Ramirez didn't want anything to happen to Deluca. They knew each other's thoughts inside and out on the cases they were working on. They always came to the same conclusions most of the time or whenever Ramirez explained the situation more thoroughly to Deluca. This did not mean that Deluca did not come up with the conclusion on the case. He was very good on details, details, and more details.

Ramirez's husband Bernie is tall and thin, also with brown eyes and brown hair. He understood his wife's job. He was also very close to Deluca. They were friends. Bernie, Rosie's husband, went through all the divorce procedures with Deluca. Bernie knew Deluca from the work they both did together on some of the cases that they had been working on. Deluca worked on a case with Ramirez, and Bernie reported the same case for the Sun Paper. In fact, Deluca was the person who introduced Bernie to Rosie. He knew Rosie was lonely and always wanted to meet someone nice. This made Ed go to work to bring both of them together. Ed knew Bernie usually went to a bar in Fells Point called "The Horse you came in on." The "Horse you came in on" is a very famous bar. It was the last place Edgar Allen Poe was in before he passed away. It is one of the most historical bars in Fells Point.

After work one evening, Ed suggested that he and Rosie go there for a drink. While they were at the bar for a while Bernie came in from a long day of working at the Sun Paper. He was exhausted from his job. His boss was on him to get the story out before the next day's paper came out. This is why he had to work so late in the evening.

Therefore, their chance meeting was set; now all Ed had to do was get Bernie and Rosie close. After a few drinks Ed told Rosie he was going home. This left Bernie and Rosie together in the bar. While they were there together, they both found out that they had many things in common with each other. So one thing led to another and the two of them decided they wanted to spend more time together.

One date led to another date and after several of months of spending many evenings together, Bernie popped the question to Rosie. He asked her if she would consider marrying him.

Rosie's answer was, "I thought you were never gonna ask me."

Because of their closeness, Bernie asked Ed to be his best man at their wedding.

After this, the three of them became close forever. They had been together for many years since the night Ed brought Rosie and Bernie together. Rosie often sends meals home to Ed because she knew he never ate properly. She always took care of Ed because of what he did for her by bringing her and Bernie together.

Deluca was such a lucky guy. Besides his partner sending food over to him, he also had a wonderful sister named Paula, who watched out for him. Paula was medium height with beautiful brown hair and blue eyes. After she took care of her family she would then make sure her brother was taken care of also. She called him all the time to check up on him.

Paula made him her famous eggplant Parmesan and took it over to his apartment. She knew he hardly ever got a decent meal. He would always eat carry out, mostly Chinese, and this worried Paula a great deal. She loved him very much and she knew he has a dangerous job. She was a true Italian woman, worried sick over her brother.

CHAPTER SIX
The Date

This case has thrown both of the detectives for a loop. They only have one person of interest but they cannot find him. One woman was injured in East Baltimore, and the other woman was injured in Glen Burnie outside of the MVA building. They have no idea what the connection was. They didn't get the connection until another woman was found injured inside the Fort McHenry's grounds. Then they found out that all the three women who were injured were all related through marriage. They were all related to the wealthy people who lived in East Baltimore.

In the meantime, Deluca wanted to see more of Helen. He thought she was very interesting. She had worked at the MVA for many years and she had progressed in all the years that she had worked there. This was the first woman who had ever struck up an interest in him in all the years that he had been separated from his wife Grace. He finally built up his nerve to call her once again and ask her for a date to take her to dinner.

Deluca checked out all the restaurants that were in her area. He wanted the place to have good food and was also a nice enough place to take someone on a first date. He found a restaurant called The Washington Station. He thought the restaurant would be perfect for their date. The restaurant was also located close to where Helen lived.

Helen was also intrigued by Deluca. When he called her she was excited to hear from him again. First they started to talk about the case. After they talked about the case for a while, Deluca asked her if she was feeling better. He told her she had experienced such a terrible ordeal, and he was worried about her.

At this time Ed finally switched the conversation and started talking about her. He asked her what her likes and her dislikes were. After a lengthy conversation, he finally asked her what he wanted to ask her from the beginning of their conversation. He hesitantly stopped the petty talk and got his nerve up to ask her if she would consider going out to dinner with him. She was surprised when he asked her this and that he was that interested in her. She was also very delighted to accept his invitation. She had been interested in him ever since the first time they met. He was very excited to ask her out and when he finally did this he couldn't believe she accepted his invitation.

Deluca asked Helen if she thought The Mount Washington Station would be okay with her to go to dinner there. Helen told him that it would be just fine with her. Deluca then asked her what time would be convenient with her for him to pick her up. Helen said around seven o'clock would be just fine with her. As their conversation was coming to an end, the date and time was finally set for their first date.

Deluca was very excited to date Helen so he made sure he was clean shaven for their meeting and dressed properly. His partner Rosie helped him pick out his outfit to wear for the evening. Rosie was so excited for Ed. She was happy he was going to be in the company of a nice woman for a change.

When he came to Helen's home he was a nervous wreck. This was the first time he had been on a date in years. After she opened her door, he couldn't believe how beautiful she looked. She had different clothes on than she wore to work. She had a beautiful blue dress on. Her hair was done up so pretty that she looked radiant. Deluca was even more delighted when he saw her looking so beautiful. He still couldn't believe she accepted his invitation to go out with him on this evening.

As they arrived at the restaurant they were greeted by a hostess who seated them at a corner table in a little secluded area. Even thought the table was in the corner it was also near the bar, this suited Ed just fine. He wanted to be able to talk to Helen and not have people listening to their conversation. Even though Ed was not working you might have thought he was. He wanted to make sure they were not interrupted by anyone this evening.

When they were seated, the waitress approached the table and greeted them. She asked them if they would like to have something to drink. Ed looked at Helen and asked her if she would like to have a glass of wine or a drink. Helen told him she would like to have a glass of wine. Then the waitress asked her what kind of wine would she like. Helen told her she would like a glass of Merlot. Then the waitress asked Ed what he would like to drink and he told the waitress he would take a beer. She asked him what kind of beer would he like and he told her a Bud Lite would be just fine for him.

Deluca told the waitress they were not in any hurry, and if she didn't mind could she please take her time. After the drinks arrived the waitress waited a while before she approached the table again. At the time she came back to the table she asked them if they were ready to order. Deluca told the waitress they had been talking so much they hadn't even looked at the menu yet. Deluca asked the waitress if she could please give them some more time. The waitress told them she would give them a few more minutes. The waitress said if they needed any help deciding what to order she would be glad to help them. They told the waitress they would try to decide because their menu looked so good.

As soon as the waitress returned to their table they ordered the Jumbo Lump Crab Wontons for appetizers. In a while the waitress returned with the appetizers. They were delicious, they both enjoyed them immensely. Later the waitress came back to the table and asked them if they were ready to order and they said yes they were. Then she cleared their table by taking the appetizer plates away. They told the waitress the menu looked so good that they were having a hard time choosing the food they wanted to eat. Helen ordered the Chicken Piccata for dinner and Ed ordered the Parmesan Crusted Wild Rockfish.

In a while the waitress returned with their dinner. When she placed their dinner in front of them she asked them if they would like something else to drink. They ordered another glass of Merlot and another Bud lite. The food looked so good they almost didn't want to bite into it. They were also a little self-conscious to start eating but eventually they finally did. The chicken was so delicious, and the sauce that it was in was fabulous. Deluca told the waitress the fish was flakey and melted in his mouth.

Next the waitress came back and asked them how everything was. They told the waitress everything was just fine. The portions were so large they couldn't finish their dinner. Of course they were so engrossed in each other's conversation they really didn't eat much of their food. They were just happy being in each other's company. They had so much to talk about because it was their first date.

Ed told Helen he worked so many hours that by the time he was finished for the day he was usually so tired to go any place to meet someone. He told Helen after working on a case all day he just wanted to go some place and have a few beers and then go home.

They asked the waitress if she would mind wrapping their food for them. She took the plates away and then when she returned with their food she asked them if they would like to have some dessert. They told her to please give them a minute, and she did. As soon as the waitress returned they told her they would both have some coffee and split a piece of cheese cake.

Helen told Ed about her experiences of dating men. She told Ed that all of them had turned into disastrous events. She told Ed this was the reason why she didn't date that much. She didn't want to experience anymore disappointments.

The evening went just fine, they had a wonderful time together and the dinner was very good. Deluca made sure that he didn't drink too much. He was really interested in Helen. He didn't want to mess anything up. After they left the restaurant, Deluca took Helen home. When they got to his car he opened the door for her to let her enter his car.

After they returned to Helen's home, he walked her to her front door. He turned her around towards him and looked into her eyes. He asked her if she had a good time and would it be okay if he saw her again. Helen told him that would be nice. Then Ed took Helen in his arms and held her close to him. He looked into her eyes and leaned towards her. He put his lips on hers. He gave her a kiss that seemed to last forever. He was very interested in her. The kiss he gave Helen made her head spin. It was such a fabulous kiss that it made her want to see him again. The kiss left her breathless. Helen was so impressed by the way he treated her and realized that she was really interested in this person. She had never been in the company with such a genuinely nice person before. This was something that she had been looking forward to for some time. Helen always wanted to find someone who really cared about her. After this fabulous kiss they both agreed that another date would be just fine with both of them. This was the beginning of a beautiful relationship.

CHAPTER SEVEN
Fort McHenry

The flag always flies over the Fort. The flag is a reminder of our nation's history. Fort McHenry is the birthplace of our National Anthem and has been visited by people from all over the world. Fort McHenry withstood the attempt by the British to capture it during the years of 1812 through 1814.

There were many ships in the water near the Fort during the war of 1812. Francis Scott Key was on one of the ships while the attack on the Fort began. Francis Scott Key was trying to help his friend Dr. William Beanes out. Dr Beanes was being held a prisoner on the flag ship of truce. During the battle, Francis Scott Key saw the rockets' red glare and the bombs bursting in air. This is what gave him the idea to pen the words that became our

National Anthem. Because of these heroic events, Fort McHenry is the very historic symbol of our heritage.

Although on this day, there was a flurry of police activity going on there. The police were called when one of the guards from the Fort discovered a woman there. She had been brutally beaten. The woman was half clothed and beaten on the left side of her head. Through the grace of God the woman survived this brutal attack on her body. This awful attack on the woman must have happened during the evening. The woman had been lying there for some time unconscious until the guards from the Fort found her. The woman was beaten the same way as the other women in East Baltimore were. She was hit with a weapon, a fist, or a rock on the right side of her head. These incidents were baffling the police. Why were these people being singled out?

The detectives Deluca and Ramirez were called in for this incident again. They had been working on all the other incidents that happened recently. They were trying to piece things together. What they found out was the two women were related to the Del Judajeas. As soon as the detectives found this out they went back to East Baltimore to question the couple again.

When the detectives came to the street that the Del Judajeas lived on, the Baltimore Gas and Electric Company was working on Bank Street. The BG&E people were tearing the street up because they were installing a new system in the area. The detectives had a hard time getting up the street because of this. After they found a place to park they went to the Del Judajea's home. When the Del Judajeas came to their door the detectives asked them if they could come in. They told them they had some questions to ask them. The detectives were very polite to the Del Judajeas.

The family of the injured women could not understand why these women were being hurt. They were very upset when they found out what happened to their nephews' wives. The Del Judajeas helped the injured women more than the women would have ever expected them to do. Even though the women were divorced from the Del Judajea's relatives, they still considered them to be part of their family. They knew the women were hard-working women, and they were trying to keep their little family together. The Del Judajeas knew all these things about the women. They knew they had small children to take care of. Therefore they made the children come to their home to live until their mothers would be able to come out of the hospital. The woman who was found at Fort McHenry name was Patricia. Her ex-husband's name was Alfredo.

Philomena invited the detectives into her kitchen. She asked them if they would like some coffee. They thanked her and told her they were okay. At this time the detectives started to talk to them about all the construction that was going on outside of their home. The detectives asked the Del Judajeas if it had affected them in anyway. Then the detectives changed their minds and told Philomena that they would take some coffee. The detectives wanted to make Philomena comfortable so when they started to ask them some questions she would not be startled.

The detectives told them about their other relative who was found in Fort McHenry. The detectives asked them if there was something that they weren't telling them. They wanted to know why all these women who were being hurt were related to them. They wanted to know what the connection was. They could not believe it was just a coincidence that they were all related to them. The detectives didn't mention explicit things to them. The detectives kept the conversation vague. They didn't insinuate that they thought the Del Judajeas had anything to do with the things that were happening to their relatives. The detectives knew the Del Judajeas were both very interested in their relatives' well being.

The Del Judajeas told the detectives they were upset about all these terrible things happening to their relatives. They told the detectives they were trying to do everything they could do to help the woman out. They told the detectives they were taking care of their children. They knew there was no one else who would be able to do this for them. They took the children into their home. They knew the woman would be in the hospital for some time. What were the children going to do in the meantime? Having the children living in their home it made it easier for the children to go to school in the area.

Philomena was very happy to be able to care for the children. She was happy to be able to cook for the children and clean their clothes. This was something she loved to do. She did not complain because she wanted to help the children. Her home was full of children again and this was something she was very happy about.

The detectives wanted to let the Del Judajeas know it would be to their advantage if they could find out who was doing this to their relatives. The detectives wanted to let them know if they didn't talk to them that something worse could happen. The detectives told the Del Judajeas if they didn't talk to them they might lose the opportunity to help them find out who the person was that was hurting their relatives. The detectives wanted the Del Judajeas to believe that it was urgent for them to help them find the person or persons who were doing this to their relatives.

The detectives wanted to make it personal and to their advantage if they helped them with this case. When the detectives couldn't get any answers from the Del Judajeas, the detectives decided they were going to take them downtown.

This made Philomena extremely nervous and upset. She didn't know what was going to happen to them. She didn't know what her husband was doing lately. She was very suspicious of his every move. She had to go along with what her husband told the detectives but she was unsure of anything that he said lately. Philomena had been receiving anonymous letters recently telling her that her husband was seeing another woman. She had become distraught about this. She had never for one minute believed her husband didn't love her anymore.

Philomena could not understand these letters she had been receiving. Who was the person that was sending them to her? Philomena didn't want to believe that they were true. Even though she and her husband were older, they still cared a great deal about each other. She believed that he loved her. He was very affectionate towards her. He always kissed her when he came home. There was never a smell of another woman on him. She could not understand if there was any truth in these letters. She wondered who was behind the letters and what this person knew that she didn't.

In the meantime, the Captain called the detectives and told them that the first woman, Nancy, who was brutally beaten was getting better. She was out of intensive care now. The Captain told the detectives he wanted them to go and interview the woman who had been hurt. The detectives took the Del Judajeas to the police station before they went to see the victim. They put the Del Judajeas in separate rooms and left them there. Then they went to interview the first victim.

CHAPTER EIGHT
Questioning the Victims

On their way over to Johns Hopkins hospital the detectives started talking about the case. They said the case was not making any sense. They couldn't figure out the connection between the women and the Del Judajeas.

As soon as the detectives arrived at the hospital, they asked the nurses to direct them to the room of the woman who was badly beaten. They had many questions for her. The nurse took them to the woman's room. When they entered the room they greeted the first victim, Nancy, and asked her how she was feeling.

Nancy had long blonde hair and was very well built. She was able to comb her hair and put a little make up on before the detectives arrived. Nancy was feeling much better and she wanted to make herself look a little more presentable if anyone came in to visit her. The doctors told Nancy she would be going home soon. She was very enthusiastic when they told her this. She was anxious to see her children.

Before the detectives started to question her they noticed the part of her face where she had been hit was starting to heal. The doctors had to shave the one side of her head that she was beaten on so they could stitch her up. Her hair had not grown back yet on that side of her head. How she was able to withstand this assault was unbelievable. The detectives both thought she must have been a very brave person.

The detectives heard that Italian people were very strong, but what she had endured was miraculous. The detectives thought she must have fought her predator off as much as she could. The one side of her head must have been where he dragged her to get her to talk to him.

The detectives asked the women how she was feeling. Then the detectives got down to business. The first question they asked her was did she know the person who attacked her. She told them she did not know who he was. She told the detectives she was getting off of work and she only wanted to get home to her children. She told the detectives she had a babysitter and didn't want to have to pay her more than she already had to.

Nancy told the detectives as she was walking home from work she could feel she was not alone. There was no one around because where she lived was a residential area. The area had all working class people. Everyone who lived in the area was asleep by this time of night. This made her feel very alone.

She turned around to see if anyone was following her but when she looked behind her she saw no one. The feeling she had made her very uncomfortable. She definitely felt the presence of someone behind her. She started to walk a little faster.

As soon as she turned around to look she saw a tall man behind her. Nancy said this man came from out of nowhere. She said she started to run to try to get away from him, but he was taller and faster than she. Nancy said when he caught up to her he kept threatening her. Her assailant kept asking her where the money was. She told her assailant she didn't have any money.

He said, "Not your money."

She said, "I don't know what you are talking about."

At first she thought he was talking about her boss, because

she worked at the strip club.

She said, "I told him I only work there. I don't know anything about his personal things."

Then he said, "No, not your boss's money your relative's money. Where do your relatives hide their money?"

She kept telling him she didn't know what he was talking about.

He kept saying to her, "Yes you do. You practically live there. Don't tell me you don't know where their money is." He told her if she didn't tell him where they hide the money he was really going to hurt her. She kept telling him she didn't know where their money was. Even though she told him this he kept questioning her over and over again.

She said, "I told him I think they keep it in the bank. I told him they have a bank account at one of the local banks here." She told him, "I think it's in the Old Line Bank." She told him, "That's where all the Italian people from Highlandtown go." As she told him this she realized it wasn't enough for him. He just kept hitting me over and over again. He kept saying, "You crazy bitch, you know where they keep their money – you're always at their house."

She told the detectives she told the man her relatives didn't discuss their personal business with her. She said whatever they do is their business not hers. She told the detectives the man didn't believe her. He kept hitting her and he kept asking her over and over again the same question. Every time he asked her this question and she said she didn't know, he kept hitting her. He kept telling her she knew where they kept their money. "Over and over again I told him I didn't know but he just kept hitting me every time I told him this."

Next the detectives asked her if she would be able to describe him if they put him in a line-up. She told the detectives she would do her best to describe the man for them. They also asked her, if they brought a person into her room to draw the face of the person who attacked her, would she be able to do this. They wanted to know if she could describe what the person looked like. She agreed to do this for them.

They told Nancy if she could describe this person for them it would help them to be able to find the person. The detectives called their sketch artist, Erin, while they were in her room. They asked Erin to come to the hospital and get a description of the person who attacked the women. They set up an appointment for Erin to come in and talk to Nancy to try to get the description of the man.

Nancy then asked the detectives how her children were. The detectives told Nancy the neighbors and their relatives the Del Judajeas were taking care of them. They told Nancy the neighbors were even collecting money for her. That way when she comes home she will have some money.

Nancy was so happy when they told her this. She thought it was very nice of her neighbors to do this for her. The detectives told her the beauticians from the beauty shop she went to also were taking up a collection for her. They said the owners of the beauty shop, Phyllis and Clara, started this collection for her. Nancy could not believe what her friends were doing for her. She knew she wouldn't be able to go back to work until her bruises were all healed.

After the detectives set up an appointment for Erin to come to Nancy's room, they said their good byes to Nancy. They told her they would get back to her at a later date. Before they left though, they gave her their card. They told her to please get in touch with them if she could think of anything else that would be important for them to hear.

In the meantime the second victim was coming around so the detectives went to talk to her also. This victims name was Patricia, and oddly enough she was also related to the rich people from East Baltimore. The detectives called Captain Dave and told him that Nancy was okay now and she would be able to describe the person who hurt her. The Captain thought that after Erin went to see Nancy she would be able to get a description of the predator.

CHAPTER NINE
The Investigation Continues

After the detectives left Johns Hopkins Hospital they went back to the police station on Eastern Avenue to question the Del Judajeas. Deluca and Ramirez put the Del Judajeas in different rooms. They wanted to make sure each of them would not know what the other one was saying.

At that time they went to talk to Carmen. They first asked him if he wanted anything to drink or eat. Carmen told them he would like to have a soda to drink. Ed got a soda for Carmen. Then Rosie read Carmen his rights because they wanted him to know he had the right to remain silent. She also told him he had the right to acquire a lawyer and if he didn't have one, they would appoint one for him. Carmen told Rosie he was okay, that he had a lawyer if he needed one. After several hours of interviewing, Carmen kept to his story that he didn't know why his family was being attacked like this.

The detectives left Carmen and went to interview Philomena. They also asked Philomena if she wanted anything to drink or eat. Philomena told them she would like to have a cup of coffee. Rosie went and got her a cup of coffee. Rosie also read Philomena her rights. Rosie wanted Philomena to know she could have a lawyer if she wanted one. Later after they told her this she started to become weary. She told the detectives that her husband was once involved in some shady deals. She said she didn't know exactly what was going on but she knew it was something strange. Philomena told the detectives someone was in their home. The person was screaming at her husband. As soon as this happened she knew something strange was going on. Philomena told the police that she was fearful for her husband.

She knew what happened to the women who were once married to their nephews. Rosie told Philomena it would be to her advantage if she could tell them something she remembered about that day. Rosie asked Philomena if she knew why this person was beating her relatives up.

"There has to be a connection to your husband," Rosie said.

"Don't you remember anything that might have led this man to beat up your relatives?

Philomena told the detective she had no idea why this man was doing this. She thought something like that might happen to her husband. She was worried for him.

Rosie said, "You know eventually they might come after your husband. What are you going to do if they hurt him? Who is going to help you? Suppose they come after you? What are you going to do? Who is going to protect you if your husband is not there to protect you?"

Rosie left Philomena worrying and wondering about what she said to her. As a result of the detectives talking to Philomena they found out how worried she was for her husband. Rosie then went to find out how Deluca was doing with Carmen.

Carmen had been in the other room and was being interviewed by Deluca. He had no idea what was going on with his wife. Deluca had been grilling Carmen about the women and asking him if he knew why they were being hurt. When Rosie came back in the room that Carmen was in, he thought they were going to tell him he could go home. On the contrary, they both questioned him further.

When Rosie came into the room, she stayed standing. They both kept asking Carmen what kind of business was he in. He kept insisting he didn't know what they were talking about. Carmen told the detectives he was retired. Rosie kept walking around the room while Ed was questioning Carmen. She was trying to make him nervous by doing this during the interview. Carmen didn't know which one to look at first.

The detectives told him, "There has to be some connection to you because all the women who were injured are related to you."

They kept questioning him but he wouldn't budge. Carmen kept to his story. He said his wife was old and she had been imagining things lately. The detectives left him in the room alone to think things over. After a while the detectives realized that they really had nothing to hold the two people on so they had to let them go. That was all right, because they were going to come to their home and question them more.

In the meantime Captain Dave's Secretary, Anna called the detectives and told them the second woman was recovering from her injuries, so the detectives went back to Johns Hopkins Hospital to question her. But before Ed and Rosie went there, Ed wanted to call Helen and ask her how she was. He hadn't called her in a while because he was so busy with all the incidents that were happening in the City. He wanted to get in touch with her because he really wanted to see her again.

When Ed called Helen, she was surprised to hear from him. She told Ed she was wondering how he was doing. She told Ed she had been checking the papers everyday to see if he was in there or not. Helen told Ed she figured, if his name was not in the paper, then he was okay. Ed told her this case had him and his partner so baffled, and this was the reason he hadn't called her.

He assured her it wasn't because he didn't want to talk to her.

Ed told Helen by the time he finished work for the day it was late in the evening. He knew she had to get up early in the morning and that was the reason he hadn't called her for some time. Ed asked Helen if it would be possible for him to see her again. Helen told Ed that would be nice. After they talked for a few minutes Ed told Helen he had some police business to attend to now. He told Helen he would call her later that evening and then they can set up the time for their date.

"Would that be okay with you?" Ed asked Helen.

Helen said, "Yes that would be fine," and with that, Ed planned to call Helen later that evening.

When the detectives arrived at the hospital they asked the nurses which room the second victim was in. The nurse told them where she was and the detectives walked to her room. The second woman who was injured name was Glenda. She was also once married to one of the relatives of the Del Judajeas.

As they entered Glenda's room they told her they were detectives Deluca and Ramirez, and they were investigating her case. Glenda had long red hair and blue eyes. They could tell she was very pretty despite all the bruises and scars on her face and arms. Before they started to question her they could tell she tried to fight her predator off more than Nancy did. Glenda's arm was severely bruised. They could also see that her nails were damaged. Helen from the MVA was the person who told Deluca that she had noticed the woman's nails were broken off.

After they gave their introductions to her, they started to question her. The first thing they asked her was if she knew her predator. Glenda told them she didn't know him. She told them the same exact thing that Nancy told them. She said she was getting off work and wanted to get home to her children. They were with the babysitter. She said she wanted to get there as soon as possible so she wouldn't have to pay more money to the babysitter.

Glenda told them she had been living in the Glen Burnie area for some time. She told the detectives the apartments were cheaper there. She had a job at one of the local restaurants in the area. She was working at the Olive Garden on Ritchie Highway. She was a waitress there and she was making a good living. She had two children to support. She told the detectives while walking home from work, a man came from out of nowhere and started to follow her. She told them she started to run to get away from him. She couldn't run fast enough though. He caught up to her and grabbed her.

She told the detectives he was so much taller than she. She couldn't outrun him. He kept threatening that if she didn't tell him were the money was he was really going to hurt her.

She said, "I kept asking him, what money?" She told him she didn't have any money.

He said, "Not your money, the Del Judajea's money."

She did not understand what he meant. She kept telling him,

"I don't know where their money is. I guess they put it in a bank."

She told him, "They don't tell me their personal business, and I don't ask them either."

Glenda kept telling him this, but he kept insisting she knew, so he kept hitting her over and over again. All the while he was hitting her he kept saying,

"I know you know where they keep their money. You practically live there."

She told the detectives she didn't remember anything else after that because she believed she passed out. Before she passed out though, she managed to scratch him.

Her assailant must have moved her body and put her in the back of the MVA so no one would be able to find her until the next day. He wanted to leave her there because he thought she might die.

Even though Glenda was injured badly she is a very strong person. She survived the assault that she endured the night before. She even survived the cold air of the evening. It is a miracle that she was able to survive. Then they asked Glenda if she could describe her assailant. She told them that she would do her best. They set up an appointment for the sketch artist, Erin to come to visit Glenda and get a description of her assailant.

As soon as they said their goodbyes and wished Glenda well they left and went to see the forensic people. They wanted to find out if the forensic people found any evidence from under Glenda's finger nails. She had scratched her assailant so hard she even broke her fingernails.

Deluca and Ramirez went to talk to their friend Brian who worked at the forensic lab. Brian always took his time. He cared about the details on every case he worked on. He took his time on everything he did because he wanted to be certain he had it right. They asked Brian if he was able to acquire any information on the assailant. Brian told Ed and Rosie that the details of any case are the most important part of the case. Brian told the detectives this is why he was taking his time. Brian was trying to sew up every detail that he could. Therefore there would not be any doubt from the evidence he had found for the detectives. Brian made sure of this before he presented the evidence to them. Brian told both of the detectives he found something but he didn't know if it was enough for them to get anything out of what he found.

Brian told the detectives the skin that the woman scraped from her predator's arm was good. He was able to get samples of his blood. The blood samples he received enabled the detectives get a complete description of the man.

Brian told the detectives, "The man is known in this area as a heavy gambler. There is nothing in particular that this man has done that would enable you detectives to lock this person up. The only thing is, if the women can identify him in a line up, then you can hold him for the crimes of assault he inflicted on these women."

The detectives were so happy after they found out this information. They finally had something to go on.

They took the information that Brian gave them and put it in their database. After they entered the information in the database, they were able to come up with some information on this person. Although they were not sure that it would be enough for them to get a description of the person, they were successful. Now all they had to do was locate this person.

The detectives got in contact with Erin, the sketch artist, and asked her to bring them the sketches she got from the two victims. When they put the likeness that Erin gave them together with the evidence that Brian gave them, they were able to get a description of the predator.

After this, Deluca had a few minutes so he called Helen. He wanted to ask her when she would be available to go out with him again. Helen was happy that Ed called her to set up their second date.

Ed told Helen, "Anyway, let's get back to you and me."

Ed wanted to find out when he could see her again. He told her he missed her. Ed told Helen he really meant to call her for some time but this case was keeping him extremely busy.

Ed asked Helen if she would like to go out to dinner on Saturday evening. Helen said that would be lovely, but where were they going to meet? Ed told Helen he would like to pick her up at her home if that would be okay with her. Helen said that would be just fine with her. Ed asked Helen what would be a good time for their meeting because they were both off on Sunday.

While talking to Helen he told her he considered his profession to be a very respectable one. This is the reason why he became a cop in the first place. He believed if he could help one person out a year he was doing his job. Ed told Helen that at first his job was fun and exciting, but this case had thrown him and his partner for a loop. Ed told Helen this job always keeps his adrenaline running.

He told Helen he still enjoys his job. The only thing he doesn't like is that the politics keep getting in the way. He also told her, he thought he could make a difference. He said the only thing wrong with his job is that he doesn't have much time for his personal life.

After he told Helen all of this, they set the time for their next date to be seven o'clock on Saturday evening. With everything set for their second date, Ed said goodbye to Helen and told her that he would see her on Saturday evening.

Now it was time to get back to work. Since they were unsuccessful with their effort to get more information from the Del Judajeas, the detectives were forced to let them go back to their home. The detectives accompanied them there. Now Mrs. Del Judajea was in her glory because she had all the children to cook for. She was anxious to be able to do this for the children. She had all the modern cooking equipment at her disposal to use. The one thing that made her happy was to be able to cook for many people again.

CHAPTER TEN
The Letters

Carmen and Philomena spent the evening together on their balcony. They would sit out on their balcony during the summer months. They liked to watch the moon and the stars. Carmen would reminisce about all the hard times he had getting her father to allow him be able to see her. Their balcony was located right outside of their bedroom. After spending a lovely evening together, Philomena started to receive letters in the mail addressed to only her. When she opened the letters she could not believe what she was reading. The letters insinuated that her husband Carmen was seeing a woman when he went out.

The letters kept coming to Philomena, one a week. Each week they had more and more detail in them. The letters told Philomena that when Carmen went out he was going to meet a woman. The letters began to describe their meeting in the different locations in Baltimore. When Carmen went out one day he told Philomena he was going over to Canton to meet one of his men.

Soon after Carmen left Philomena received another letter. The letter told her that Carmen was going to meet his girlfriend in Canton. Then the next week he told Philomena he had to go to Fells Point to meet someone who was going to take book for him there. As soon as Carmen left Philomena received another letter telling her that Carmen was meeting his girlfriend in Fells

Point. This really upset Philomena. It appeared that this person had some device set up in their home that knew Carmen's every move. Then the next day Philomena received another letter. The letter told her that Carmen was going out to meet the woman again.

When these letters kept coming, Philomena became more and more on edge. She had never doubted her husband before this. She believed he was truthful to her. In all the years that they had been together he had never cheated on her, not once.

The letters made Philomena become suspicious and sharp towards her husband. On one occasion Carmen told her he was going out to meet one of his workers. She would snap at him and say, "Yes I'm sure you're going out to meet one of your workers." Carmen would look at her, and wonder what was wrong with Philomena.

A few days later, Carmen went out and Philomena received another letter. The letter stated Carmen was going out to meet his lover. Philomena became distraught. She could not believe this was happening to her. They had been together for fifty years. Philomena thought, "Why now?" In spite of all these years of being together, Philomena wondered what was going on.

Philomena had no one to confide in. All of Philomena's in-laws were Italian. They would all be on Carmen's side. Philomena only spoke to her neighbors to say hello. She would have a friendly conversation with them but nothing about her family. Philomena needed someone that she could confide in. Finally she called her oldest friend Rita. She knew that Rita was the only person she would be able to talk to about this. She called her and asked Rita if she could meet with her someplace close to her home. Rita told Philomena they could meet at one of the restaurants near her home. Philomena told Rita that would be fine. Then they said their good byes and said they would see each other tomorrow.

The next day Philomena told Carmen she was going to meet her girlfriend Rita for lunch. Carmen said, "That's a shame, I was going to take you to our favorite restaurant in Little Italy for lunch." Philomena told Carmen, "We can go there another day." Philomena told Carmen she hadn't seen her girlfriend Rita in such a long time and that they had a lot to catch up on. With this Carmen agreed to take Philomena out to lunch another day.

Carmen told her he was going out to lunch with Rudolpho. Carmen told Philomena, "We have some business to talk about." After he left, Philomena received another letter. This letter stated that Carmen was going to meet his girlfriend. As soon as Philomena received this letter she began to cry. What was she to do? It took a while for her to control herself. When she was finally able to do this she got herself ready to go and meet her friend Rita for lunch. They met for lunch at the White Marsh Mall. They both decided to go to the Olive Garden because they both liked Italian food.

When they met, Philomena hugged Rita and kissed her on the check. She thanked Rita for meeting with her. Then they were seated and the waitress came over to their table and asked them if they would like to have something to drink. They both told the waitress they would like to have a glass of Merlot. Then Philomena started to tell Rita all the things that were happening to her. She told Rita that she didn't know what to do or who to turn to. Philomena told Rita she was beside herself. She told Rita that she was the only true friend she had. She knew she could talk to her and there would not be any hostility. Philomena also told Rita that she couldn't talk to Carmen's relatives. Philomena told Rita they are all Italian and they would all be on Carmen's side.

Rita could not believe what she was hearing. Rita told Philomena out of all the people that she knew she believed their marriage was solid as a rock. Rita told Philomena she could call her anytime she needed to talk to someone. Rita said that she would be there for her whenever she needed her. As a result of their talk they had a nice lunch together and agreed to see each other again.

A week later Carmen told Philomena he wanted to take her out to lunch at their favorite restaurant in Little Italy. This made Philomena happy. They always had a good time while they were there. As they arrived at the restaurant, the owner's children, Phil and Lisa, seated them at their favorite table. The reason they liked this table was because you could see who was seated in the restaurant.

When they were seated the waitress came over to the table and asked them if they would like something to drink. The waitress who was serving them was short and thin and she had long red hair. Carmen told the waitress they would like some iced tea. Philomena became a little uneasy. She started to wonder if this waitress was the person her husband was seeing.

All of these thoughts started Philomena's head to spin. As soon as the waitress came back with the iced teas she told the waitress she had changed her mind. She told the waitress she wanted a glass of Merlot. Carmen looked at Philomena and said, "You never drink during the day. Are you okay?" Philomena told Carmen she was perfectly fine. But each time the waitress came back to their table she became more belligerent towards her. Later when the waitress came back to the table she told the waitress she wanted another glass of Merlot. Carmen said, "What's the matter with you today, why are you acting this way?" Philomena would not answer him.

Finally their food came and they began to eat their lunch. When Philomena ordered her third glass of Merlot, Carmen told the waitress to please bring him the check. On the way home

Carmen asked Philomena, "What's wrong with you?"

Philomena told Carmen, "You are what's wrong with me." Philomena asked him, "Who have you been seeing behind my back? After all these years aren't I enough for you anymore? You have to go elsewhere to be satisfied?"

Carmen was shocked. He said, "What are you talking about?"

Philomena said, "You know exactly what I am talking about. Why are you seeing this other woman? Do you want a divorce?"

Carmen was dumbfounded and replied, "What are you talking about?"

When she answered this question, he believed the wine was taking effect. Philomena told Carmen, "I know you have been seeing someone else. People have been telling me."

Carmen said, "Who has been telling you these lies? I have never cheated on you in all the years we have been together." He also said, "After the hard time I had to convince your parents to let me see you, why would you think I was cheating on you now?"

Philomena told him, "People have been telling me this."

Carmen asked again, "Who is telling you these lies?" Philomena told Carmen, "I have been receiving letters. Every letter I received told me this. They all said when you go out you are going to meet your lover."

This upset Carmen so much, he said, "That's a bold ass lie. I have never cheated on you. I am going to get to the bottom of this." When he got Philomena home, he called Rudolpho and told him he had to see him and to please come over to his home.

When Rudolpho arrived at Carmen's home, Carmen told him everything that Philomena told him. Carmen told Rudolpho, "We have got to get to the bottom of this. Someone is trying to break Philomena and me up. I don't understand this at all."

Rudolpho told Carmen, "The only thing that I know is that the Little Italy bookies are upset with you because you don't want to sell drugs. But I don't have any idea who is doing this to you."

"There is another issue I have to talk to you about. We will get to that after we find out about what is happening to Philomena."

Earlier, Carmen made a great offer to Rudolpho because he had been close to Carmen for years. Rudolpho knew just about everything about Carmen and his family and he knew Carmen was a good person.

As soon as Carmen told Rudolph about what was happening to Philomena, he jumped right on it. Rudolpho told his guys what was happening. Rudolpho got his men to go out and find out about these accusations as soon as possible. They put their feelers out there to find out who was causing all this aggravation for Carmen and Philomena. Carmen was Rudolpho's closest friend and he certainly didn't want him to have all this aggravation in his life now that he was considering retiring.

Rudolpho's men went to the places where all the smaller bookies hung out. They thought by mingling with them they could find out what was going on. After many visits with these people, going to all the little bars and restaurants they hung out in, they found out the culprit was Donald. He was the person who was creating all this havoc for Carmen and Philomena. Donald wanted to make Carmen's life miserable because he still believed Carmen owed him money. Rudolpho found this out and he sent his guys to look for Donald. Of course no one had seen or heard from him for some time. Donald was lying low because he knew people were looking for him.

CHAPTER ELEVEN
Second Date

Because Ed had to work so much on the case, he wanted to make sure that the next meeting with Helen would be a memorable one. He decided to take Helen to his favorite Italian restaurant, the famous Sabatino's restaurant in Little Italy.

The restaurant had been established in Little Italy for over fifty years. This restaurant has been visited by many movie stars, singers, football players, baseball players, basketball players, and many local celebrities. It was also visited by many judges, district attorneys, police detectives, and local lawyers in Baltimore.

There was a very quiet table up in the mezzanine, which is a private section of the restaurant. Deluca picked Helen up around 7 o'clock so they would be able to have a nice dinner together. Deluca didn't want Helen to drive. They arrived at the restaurant around seven thirty, and they were greeted by Vince, one of the owners, and Renato Jr., the son of the other owner. Vince and Renato knew Deluca because he came into the restaurant frequently to get their fabulous bookmaker salad. That was Deluca's favorite thing to order at lunch time.

Deluca made a reservation to make sure he would be able to get the special table at this certain time in the evening. He also requested his favorite waitress, Lynn. As soon as they were seated Lynn came over to the table to great them. She asked them how they were both doing this evening. Lynn knew Deluca because

The People of Sabatino's

he frequented the restaurant during lunch. Lynn asked both of them if they would like to have anything to drink before dinner. They told Lynn yes they would like to have a drink before dinner. Ed ordered a glass of Merlot for Helen and a Bud Lite for himself. When Lynn arrived with their drinks she asked them if they wanted to wait a few minutes before they ordered. They told her, "Yes we would like to wait... is that okay Lynn?" Lynn agreed and gave them some time to themselves.

While they were alone they began to talk about what was happening in each of their lives. Helen told Ed that things were finally getting back in order down at the MVA. She told Ed that people were starting to come back there, even after all the bad publicity the MVA had received. Ed told Helen he had been meaning to call her for some time but every time he had a free minute something else had developed with the case. He told Helen, "You have been on my mind ever since our last date." Ed told Helen that he made sure that he was able to find the time to get in touch with her to ask her out. Helen was very happy to hear Ed say this. After their first date she wanted to see him again. She told Ed she thought he had forgotten about her. Ed assured her that he could not forget about her. She was constantly on his mind. Ed told Helen this case was consuming all of his time.

Lynn returned to the table to ask them if they were ready to order. Ed asked Lynn, "How about a couple of appetizers first?" He ordered the Shrimp Renato and fresh Mozzarella, tomatoes and basil for their appetizers. Lynn told him that would be just fine and she went to put their orders in the kitchen. While they were there alone Ed took Helen's hand and told her how much he missed her. He apologized for not calling her sooner. Helen told Ed that now she understood it was his job. She assured him not to worry. She was not angry with him. Soon Lynn returned with the appetizers.

Helen told Ed she had never had the Shrimp Renato before and she enjoyed it very much. Ed told Helen this dish was created when little Renato was born. They were having such a wonderful time just being able to talk to one another alone. Soon Lynn came back to take their order. Ed told Lynn they were going to have two Veal dishes. Ed ordered the Veal Francese for their dinner. Lynn told them they had to choose salad or pasta. Ed asked Helen what she would like. She told Ed she would like a salad. Ed told Lynn he would take a salad also.

Soon Lynn was back with their salads served with the restaurant's famous house dressing. After they finished their salads Lynn returned to take them away. Lynn didn't want to rush them because Ed told her in advance that he was bringing someone he was really interested in to the restaurant. Lynn gave Ed and Helen time to talk to one another.

Helen told Ed about her life and why she was alone. She told him she had many disappointments in her life. She told Ed she was leery of starting a relationship with another man because she didn't want to be disappointed again. Ed told Helen he would try his best not to disappoint her. Ed told her if she would be able to go along with his crazy schedule he would not do anything to hurt her. Helen was very happy to hear this because she really wanted to be with him. Helen thought he was a very exciting person.

Soon Lynn came back with their dinner and she asked them if they would like to have another drink. They said, "Yes," so Lynn brought them two more drinks, a glass of Merlot and a bottle of Bud Lite. They had such a wonderful dinner. The Veal was very tender and the wine sauce gave the veal a special taste. Lynn could tell they wanted to talk so she left them alone and didn't go back to their table for some time. They were enjoying each other's company. They were talking so much that they could not finish their dinner. They were so engrossed in their conversation they almost forgot to eat.

Lynn came back and asked them if they wanted to take their food home and they told her yes. When she returned she asked them if they would like dessert. They told her they would have to think about it first, so Lynn gave them some more time. Later when Lynn returned she asked them if they had decided on dessert they told her that they really didn't want anything else, except two espressos. After they had the espresso Lynn brought them their check. When they left the restaurant they talked all the way to Helen's home.

As they arrived at Helen's home they decided they didn't want the evening to end so Helen asked Ed if he would like to come in for some coffee. Ed said that would be nice. Once they were in Helen's home Ed took her in his arms and gave Helen a kiss that sent her head spinning. She was not sure if it was the kiss or the wine, but she knew she enjoyed the kiss very much.

One kiss led to another and before they knew it they were in each other's arms all evening. They spent a wonderful evening together. This was something they had both wanted to do for some time. This was the beginning of a wonderful relationship together. They cared for each other very much and didn't want this evening to end.

When they got up in the morning Helen made coffee. She asked Ed if he would like something to eat. Ed told Helen that would be nice because he really didn't have to go to work this day. Helen told Ed she didn't have to go to work either so she would make them some breakfast. While Helen was trying to make breakfast Ed kept coming over to her and kissing her on her neck. Helen told him if he didn't stop that they would never have any breakfast. Ed told her that would be okay with him. Helen told Ed to please sit and wait and breakfast would be ready in a few minutes.

Helen told Ed, "I know what. Why don't you go out front and get the paper? I have the Sunday Sun Paper delivered to my home." She told Ed he could read the paper while she was preparing breakfast. Ed told her okay, he would get the paper although he would much rather be kissing her. Helen just laughed and kept preparing the breakfast while Ed went to get the paper. By the time Ed came back with the paper Helen had the breakfast almost ready. While they were eating breakfast Ed told Helen he had been meaning to tell her for some time how much he appreciated her. Ed told Helen that because she told him about the victim losing her finger nails they were able to find some DNA from under the woman's fingernails. He told Helen they found something but now they had to find the person.

As they were eating breakfast Ed kept nibbling on Helen's fingers. While he nibbled on her fingers he moved closer to her, and one thing led to another and Ed was kissing her lips once again. This was the most wonderful breakfast that each of them had ever had. They had the whole afternoon to spend with each other. This was something that they both wanted to do and definitely enjoyed very much.

After spending the better part of the afternoon in each other's arms, Ed thought he should leave so Helen could get some rest. He knew she had to be to work early in the morning. Even though neither one of them wanted to leave each other, they both thought it would be best if Ed left. They finally said their good-byes and Ed was on his way to his apartment. When Ed got home he called Helen and thanked her for the wonderful time they had together. He told her he was looking forward to seeing her again. He told her he would call her the next day. Helen told him to call her when he had a chance. With their conversation coming to an end, they both were looking forward to seeing one another again.

CHAPTER TWELVE
The Investigation Continues

W̲ith the investigation in full speed, the detectives determined that the name of the man who owned the strip club was Robert. Ed and Rosie sent floaters to the strip club to check it out. They told them to keep an eye on the owner and to get friendly with the bartender. Deluca told the floaters, "After you become friendly with the bartender then maybe you will be able to find out who the owner is gambling with." Deluca wanted to verify that the owner of the club was gambling with the Del Judajeas from East Baltimore.

Deluca had a friend whose character was a little shaky. Ed had been friends with this person ever since they were young. The man's name was Fast Eddie. Fast Eddie earned his name because before anyone could recognize him he was gone. He was thin and very fast on his feet. Because of his appearance he could get into places that the detectives could not get into without being recognized. Deluca sent his friend Fast Eddie to the bar to check out the situation.

Whenever Deluca needed special surveillance services into difficult places, he relied on Fast Eddie to do the surveillance for him. If Deluca personally went into these places people would automatically know he was a cop. Criminals could smell cops a mile away. This is why Ed relied on his friend Fast Eddie to go to the strip club to find out about the gambling activity that was going on there. Fast Eddie would be able to go there and find out things that Deluca and the other police could not. Because Fast Eddie was so thin he could be in one spot, and before anyone knew it, he could be somewhere else.

After Fast Eddie did his surveillance on the strip club, he reported back to Deluca about what he found out there. He told Deluca that the owner of the club was always on the phone talking to someone. He also told Deluca that there were a lot of TVs in the room that had college and pro games on them at all times. This gave the detectives the idea that the owner was gambling on college as well as the professional games. Fast Eddie saw how the owner Robert would become upset if the team he bet on did not win. Deluca realized that the hunch that he had about the gambling was true. Fast Eddie also told Deluca that there were a lot of weird people in the strip club but he did not see a tall man who walked with a limp in there.

When the floaters became friendly with the bartenders they came back and reported to the detectives. The floaters told the detectives that Robert, the owner of the club, was a heavy gambler. This was the same thing that Fast Eddie had told Deluca. Robert was betting on football games, and losing more and more every week. He couldn't win anything. The floaters found out that the owner was in debt way over his head. Armed with the information about the owner of the club, Captain Dave sent the police there to take Robert in for questioning.

As soon as Fast Eddie did all this surveillance for Deluca, he asked him to go to the Del Judajeas. Deluca wanted Fast Eddie to find out as much as he could about the Del Judajeas, because he thought the Del Judajeas were doing something illegal. He thought the Del Judajeas were taking bets on football games, basketball games, and numbers. Deluca told Fast Eddie to keep a log of how many people went in and out of the Del Judajea's home. Deluca thought that the Del Judajeas were behind the reason the women were getting assaulted.

Fast Eddie did exactly what Deluca told him to do. He started to watch the Del Judajea's house. Fast Eddie had a camera and took pictures of all the people who were coming and going in the Del Judajea's home. He also kept a log of the amount of time that the people stayed in the Del Judajea's home. Fast Eddie told Ed that the people didn't stay in the Del Judajea's home for a long period of time. Fast Eddie had all this information documented for Deluca.

Due to Fast Eddie's surveillance on the Del Judajea's home, he had plenty of information to give to Deluca. He had pictures of people and the times of their arrival and departure from the Del Judajea's home all documented. This was such a big help to the detectives. They finally had something to go on to bring the Del Judajeas back in for questioning.

The area where the first woman was beaten was a safe residential area. Many families lived there. This was also the area that was near the Del Judajea's home. Over the months that followed many people were questioned and leads were checked out. The leads took the police nowhere. Time and time again the police thought they had someone of interest in the case, but they couldn't come up with anything solid.

CHAPTER THIRTEEN
The Investigation Narrows

Now the detectives were even more convinced that the Del Judajeas were involved in all of the things that were happening to the women, even though they told the detectives they did not know anything about what was happening. Because the detectives found out about the gambling that was going on in East Baltimore they were more convinced that the Del Judajeas were running a huge gambling ring there. Robert, the owner of the strip bar on Pulaski Highway was brought into headquarters for questioning.

The detectives put him in a room by himself. The longer he was in there, the more nervous he became. Rosie and Ed entered the investigation room to question Robert. As the detectives entered the room they were each carrying a stack of papers. When Robert saw all those papers he became extremely nervous. They both said their "hellos" to Robert and introduced themselves to him. The detectives said to him, "I guess you were wondering why you were brought into the police department." The detectives told Robert, "You are here to answer some questions for us." They read him his rights. They told him if he needed a lawyer the court would provide one for him. Robert told the detectives that he didn't need a lawyer, he had a good one. They also asked him if he wanted anything to drink or eat. Robert told them he would like some water. They got some water for him. As they were talking to him, each one of them kept walking around the room. They were trying to make him more nervous than he already was. This tactic was definitely working on Robert. He was sweating profusely.

At this time, the detectives told Robert, "We know you are a heavy gambler. Now we want to know who you place your bets with." Robert was stuttering like crazy by now. He was afraid to open his mouth. If he told the detectives who he bet with he would get the person in trouble. But more importantly he would be implying that he was placing bets illegally.

He was stuttering all over himself, torn between his loyalty to Carmen or protecting himself. He didn't know what to do. The detectives told him, "You can either answer our questions or you can spend a couple of nights in jail. When they told him this, Robert became more nervous than ever. He was really confused. He didn't know what to do. Robert asked, "Can't I talk to someone before I answer you? Can I have a lawyer?" The detectives said, "Yes, you can have a lawyer. But remember this, though after you get a lawyer you are still going to have to answer our questions."

Robert had a lawyer who took care of his business, so he called this person. Robert called his long-time lawyer and friend Stanley Alpert. The lawyer had been Robert's lawyer for several years. Stanley knew everything about Robert that there was to know about him.

As soon as Stanley arrived at the police station on Eastern Avenue he asked the detectives if he could speak with his client alone. The detectives, Rosie and Ed told Stanley that he could do this. However, Stanley and Robert did not know that the detectives had a microphone hidden in the room.

While Stanley was talking with Robert their conversation was listened to. Robert told Stanley that he didn't know what to do. He didn't want to give the bookie up. What should he do? Stanley told Robert, "You have to save yourself now and don't worry about the bookie. I'm sure the bookie has his own lawyers." Robert asked his lawyer, "Could they get me for placing bets? This is illegal isn't it?" Stanley told Robert that if they got him on this charge it would be a misdemeanor. Stanley told Robert not to worry about this now. So with the advice the lawyer gave Robert, he decided to talk to the detectives.

As soon as the detectives heard this they decided to give Robert a little more time to think before they entered the room. They didn't want Robert to think they heard what he was saying to his lawyer.

Later when the detectives entered the room they were carrying their papers again. The detectives asked Robert, "What conclusions have you come up with? Are you ready to talk to us, Robert, or what are you going to do?"

Robert told the detectives he was ready to talk to them. When he began to talk to the detectives, Robert told them that he was placing bets with Carmen. Robert said that he was doing this through a stripper named Nancy who worked at his club. Robert told the detectives he had been betting with Carmen for some time. Robert said he liked Carmen because he was good pay. He told the detectives that when he won, Carmen paid him right away. He also told them that when he lost, Carmen wanted to get his money right away. Robert claimed that this is why they had a long relationship with one another. When Robert was finished with his story, the detectives gave him papers to fill out stating everything that he just told them.

While Robert was filling out the papers the detectives went to talk to Captain Dave. They told their Captain what was going on. The Captain said he was pleased with what they found out. He told the detectives that they now had the evidence that they have been trying to get on Carmen for some time, and to bring him in. After Captain Dave told the detectives this, it was exactly what Ed and Rosie did.

This time when the detectives arrived at the Del Judajea's home, it wasn't a bright sunny day. It was a gloomy rainy day. The weather was just perfect for the situation that was about to happen to the Del Judajeas. Carmen answered the door and when he saw the detectives again he was shocked. He asked the detectives, "What's wrong now? What do you want with us again?" Ed and Rosie told Carmen that something came up and wanted to talk to him again. Not knowing what had happened earlier in the day, Carmen led the detectives into his home. Carmen asked the detectives to come into their kitchen.

As the detectives came into the kitchen they told Carmen why they were there. Ed told Carmen they wanted him to come downtown with them. Rosie told Carmen they have something important to talk to him about. Carmen had no idea what they wanted to talk to him about because they were discreet. Carmen said his goodbyes to Philomena, thinking he would be coming home soon.

When Carmen arrived at the police headquarters the detectives put him in a room alone. Then they went to the Captain and told him that Carmen was in one of the waiting rooms. After he was there for a while they came in and started to question him again. They told Carmen they had another witness who told them he was placing bets with him. Carmen was in shock. He told the detectives he wasn't answering any of their questions. He told them he knew his rights and he insisted on talking to his lawyer Joe. The detective knew he was right, so they let him call his lawyer again.

When Joe, Carmen's lawyer, arrived at the police station, they let him in the room that Carmen was in. The detectives told the lawyer that they had a witness who told them he was placing bets with Carmen. The lawyer told the detectives, "Well that's one person against Carmen." The lawyer told the detectives that Carmen told them he didn't take book.

Thanks to Fast Eddie's surveillance, Deluca had pictures of people and their time of arrival and departure from the Del Judajea's home all documented. Rosie and Ed had been busy piecing the times and pictures together of the people who were coming and going into the Del Judajea's home. They had plenty of ammunition to question the Del Judajeas about.

The detectives told Carmen and his lawyer they had evidence of all of the people coming and going in Carmen's home.

The detectives asked Carmen, "What were all of those people doing when they entered your home?" Deluca told Carmen, "These people were only in your home for a short period of time. What were they doing when they came in your home?"

Carmen told the detectives that these people were coming to his home to offer their condolences for the girls who had been hurt.

Then Deluca asked Carmen, "How come they were only in your home for a such a short period of time?"

Carmen told the detectives, "They had things to do, that's why." Carmen told the detectives they brought gifts for the women. The detectives told Carmen they weren't carrying presents when they entered your home. Carmen told the detectives they brought money for the women.

"That's why they weren't seen carrying presents."

At this time the detectives told Carmen, "We still have the statement from a witness who told us he was placing bets with you."

Joe the lawyer told the detectives, "That's just one person's word against Carmen's." Joe told the detectives, "You have to let my client go. This is a misdemeanor," The detectives went to confer with Captain Dave as to what they should do now. Captain Dave told the detectives, "Carmen's lawyer can place bail but we are still going to watch Carmen."

Robert's lawyer, Stanley, got Robert out of the police headquarters as well. Stanley told the detectives that they were holding Robert on a misdemeanor charge so they had to let him go. When the detectives talked to Captain Dave he agreed to let Robert go too.

CHAPTER FOURTEEN
More Information Surfaces

When the detectives were informed that they couldn't keep Carmen in custody, they had no choice but to let him go. As they were releasing him, they were told by one of their fellow detectives that they should go to the hospital. The detectives were told that one of the women who were hurt was assaulted again. Someone entered the hospital and tried to harm Glenda again.

Captain Dave told the detectives to go to the hospital and see how Glenda was. When Ed and Rosie arrived at the hospital the other detectives told them that the only reason Glenda did not get hurt was because the nurses were on their usual rounds. They were getting ready to give the patient her medicine. As the nurses approached Glenda's room they heard her screaming. They ran to Glenda's room only to see the predator running past them to try to escape the hospital.

The nurses called for security but by the time the security guards arrived the predator had already escaped. The nurses got a little description of the person who tried to hurt Glenda. They told the detectives the man was very tall and he ran with a limp. They told the detectives this was why they called security because they believed the man could be caught. He eluded the security guards by telling them the person was running the other way. This enabled the predator to get out of the hospital.

The detectives talked to the security people, and they told

them what happened. The security told the detectives, by the time they found out that this man was the one who tried to hurt the patient, it was too late, and the man got away. Rosie and Ed decided to question Glenda to find out what happened.

As they entered Glenda's room, a nurse was trying to calm Glenda down. Rosie and Ed asked the nurse if they could talk to Glenda. She told them they could. The nurse cautioned them though. She told them she didn't know how long Glenda would be able to talk to them because she had given her a sedative.

Glenda told them the man came in and threatened her again. The man told her not to give any description to the police about him. He told Glenda, "If you give them the description of me, I will come back and hurt your children." Glenda was still terrified, but the sedative the nurse gave her was taking effect and she was starting to dose off.

Since the detectives were not able to get much information from Glenda, they left. Before they left though, they made sure her room was protected by a police officer. The police officer sat right outside Glenda's room, to make sure no one came in to hurt her again.

When the detectives got back to the police station, Carmen was still there. The detectives told him what happened to Glenda. They told Carmen that someone got into Glenda's room and tried to hurt her again. They told him the only thing that saved Glenda was the nurse making her rounds. The nurse heard her screaming and ran into Glenda's room. As the nurse ran into Glenda's room, she saw someone trying to assault her again.

They said to Carmen, "Is this what you want to happen to your wife?" They told Carmen that the suspect could be crazy, and he was not going to stop. Carmen began to think. While Carmen was thinking the detectives kept talking to him. They told him, "Suppose this person gets into your home while you are away and hurts your wife? Is this what you want to happen to her? Do you think he won't hurt her? This person is hurting a lot of people! What makes you think he won't hurt your wife?"

The detectives asked Carmen, "Why do you think these women were being singled out like this? The women who were beaten were poor working class people. The women worked hard because their husbands who are your blood relatives were no help to them."

Rosie said, "Come on, Carmen do you want this person to keep hurting your family? What do you think? Do you think he cares about women? Look what he did to your relatives." Everything they were saying was penetrating into Carmen's mind.

The detectives went to talk to Captain Dave. As they approached the Captain's room they were greeted by his secretary Anna. She told the detectives that the Captain would be with them momentarily. The detectives told Anna they needed to talk to him, to ask his advice on what to do now.

Anna told the detectives that the Captain was getting deluged by phone calls from politicians and reporters. Anna also told them the politicians and the reporters wanted to know how come the detectives could not find out who this person was. They were telling the Captain, "It has already been over a month and no one has caught this person yet." Anna told the detectives that the reporters were badgering the Captain. She also said this was upsetting the Captain very much. Anna told them the Captain was trying to take up for the detectives by telling the reporters how hard his detectives were working on the case. Anna told the detectives that even though the Captain was telling the reporters this, the reporters kept questioning him over and over again.

The detectives waited patiently to talk to the Captain. They did not know all these things were happening to the Captain.

When they were finally able to talk to the Captain they told him about everything that happened to Glenda. The Captain also told the detectives they did the right thing to let Carmen go.

Later, when Carmen arrived home, he immediately called his friends from Little Italy and asked them what was happening. Carmen wanted to know what was up and why these people were hurting his relatives.

Carmen said, " I have been friends with you people in Little Italy for years. Why are you all of a sudden attacking my people?" Carmen wanted to know what was going on.

Alberto and Joseph told Carmen that they did not have anything to do with this person who was hurting his relatives. They told Carmen they never told anyone to hurt his relatives. Deep down inside Carmen knew that they knew who this person was, but at this time he didn't want to start anything with them. Carmen decided to call his friend Rudolpho.

Rudolpho told him, "The people from Little Italy want you to start selling drugs."

Carmen replied to Rudolpho, "I told them I don't want to get involved in drugs. Look what happened to my nephews." Carmen kept saying, "I don't want anything to do with drugs, they are bad. Why are they insisting that I should do this? It is ridiculous."

"What does it matter to them what I do? If they want to sell drugs, let them sell drugs." Carmen told Rudolpho, "Why do I have to do what they are doing?" Carmen was very upset about this. He was dead set against drugs. Carmen saw his nephews getting involved in drugs and saw how it hurt their wives and children.

Rudolpho told Carmen, "The person who is hurting your relatives is mad with you. He believes you owe him money."

Rudolpho said, "The man said you would not pay him."

Carmen told Rudolpho, "I paid this man the money I owed him."

However, Rudolpho told Carmen, "I know what you told me but the man keeps insisting that you still owe him more money."

Carmen said, "I don't owe him any money! You know how good I am with my records. I keep great records. I believe what I gave the man was what I owed him. This man is crazy."

Rudolpho told Carmen, "I know this and you know this, but this man is still insisting that you owe him more money."

Carmen replied, "Someone has to catch this man and straighten him out. What can you do to help me Rudolpho?" Rudolpho told Carmen he would look into this matter and he would get back to him. When their conversation ended, Carmen believed that Rudolpho would do something to take care of this awful person.

Donald had been walking with a limp for several years. It stemmed from when he was young. Donald and a group of his young friends were climbing trees in Patterson Park. They were just a group of little boys hanging out in the park. They all lived in the same neighborhood of Highlandtown. They had been friends all of their lives. Donald was trying to show off to his friends as he sometimes always did. When he tried to step on a huge branch in the tree, he missed it. He fell all the way down to the ground. He hurt his leg very badly. He had to have an operation on his left leg. The limp was a result of the operation on his leg. Donald was supposed to have his leg operated on again when he got older. Since he never did this, he still walks with a limp today.

His disability caused Donald to be unable to play sports while he was young. Not being able to play sports upset him very much. This is when he started to get involved in other things. He got involved with the bookies of Highlandtown. As a young teenager, he started to run numbers for them. This was the beginning of a friendship between Donald and the bookies.

CHAPTER FIFTEEN
The Compromise

Carmen's conversation with Rudolpho convinced him that he could do something to help him. He was not aware that Rudolpho was also friends with the people from Little Italy. Carmen thought Rudolpho was his true friend, which he was. Rudolpho had ties with the bookies from Little Italy, from when he was young, but Rudolpho cared a great deal more for Carmen than he did for the bookies of Little Italy. Eventually, Carmen would find out that Rudolpho had been working for the Little Italy bookies also. Although Rudolpho was friends with Carmen for years, the people from Little Italy made him a great offer he really didn't want to turn down. He was torn between his friendship with Carmen and the offer that was put before him by the people from Little Italy. Rudolpho could not be bothered with the offer from the Little Italy bookies now. He had to do something to help his long-time friend Carmen out first.

When Carmen asked Rudolpho to find the man who was hurting his relatives, Rudolpho told Carmen he would do this for him. He made sure that he went after the man who was hurting Carmen's relatives.

Rudolpho had many people who were considered his workers, so he called on them to help him now. He put the word out to them to look for a tall thin man who walked with a limp. He told his workers that the man's name was Donald and he was a heavy gambler. Rudolpho told his men to go to all the local bars in the area and look for a man who is always playing the poker machines or betting on the horse races.

After looking in all the local bars in the area they came across a little bar in East Baltimore. The bar was in the basement of a building and was only frequented by the local people who lived in the neighborhood. They had a couple of poker machines in the back of their business. A small game of chance was near the front of the bar that people could bet on. The game had horse races and keno that were also available. The screen showed all the numbers that came up on it. If your numbers came up on the screen, you could win.

Rudolpho's men had been searching for days before they came across this small bar, in East Baltimore. They were dressed in jeans and t-shirts so they wouldn't look out of place with the other people in the area. They sat in a little area across from the bar and had two Natty Boh's. There was a man sitting at the bar playing Keno. Then the bartender asked the man if he wanted another beer. He called him Donald.

When the man got up to go to the bathroom they noticed how tall he was. Rudolpho's men thought to themselves that this could be the man they had been looking for. Then when the man came back to the bar they noticed he was limping. The limp convinced them that he was the man that they were looking for. As the man came back from the men's room, he sat down at the bar near the same machine that he was playing on before and he kept gambling. They could tell he was a huge gambler by the way he became upset if he lost. After the man kept losing money, he got disgusted and left. Rudolpho's two men followed him.

Donald walked down the street towards Greek town. The two men followed Donald. He went down the under pass which eventually leads to Greek town. The two men stayed their distance about a block away and on the other side of the street. They didn't want to be noticed. But they were close enough to watch where Donald was going. As they traveled through the under pass towards Greek town, they still kept following Donald while keeping their distance.

Donald crossed over the street and went into an open building, where all the local Greek men congregated during the day. It is called the coffee house. Most of the men who went there played cards, gambled, talked to one another, and drank espresso all day. This is why Donald fit right in with them. He knew most of the men there because he frequented this place.

Rudolpho's two men went into one of the sub shops in the area to buy sodas, so they wouldn't be so conspicuous. They were in a place in Greek town where the local people from the neighborhood hung out. The two men mingled with the locals.

After Donald was there for some time, he left the coffee house. He spent all the money he came out with this day. He was out of money now. Rudolpho's men followed him again, not knowing where he was going now. He turned down Ponca Street, where his apartment was located. The two men kept following him at a distance.

It was getting late in the day and the sun had began to set. It was getting dark when Donald got closer to his apartment. The two men approached him. They confronted him and told him they wanted to talk to him.

Donald said, "I don't know you. What do you want to talk to me about?" They grabbed the man and struggled with him. They were both huge men, so they were able to overpower Donald. They took him in the back of an alley. They asked him, "Why were you beating the women up? What was your problem?"

Donald confessed to the men that he wanted his money and

he was trying to go through the women to get it. The two men continued to beat Donald. They kept telling him to leave the women alone. They told him if he kept hurting these people he was going to be very sorry. After they finished what they had come to do, they left Donald lying in the alley, in his blood, in the back of his apartment.

Rudolpho's men told Donald to leave Del Judajea's family alone, or else, he would be getting more of the same.

When they left Donald, he crawled to his apartment. The people who lived in the neighborhood did not want to get involved in this situation, as they knew better. None of the people who lived in the area came out to investigate what was going on, they only peered out of their windows. They didn't do anything to help the man out because they didn't want to get involved.

The two men reported back to Rudolpho what they did to the man. They also told Rudolpho that they told Donald to leave Carmen's family alone or else more of the same would happen to him. Rudolpho was pleased with what his men told him.

Rudolpho called Carmen and told him he should not have any more trouble with this man that was hurting his relatives. Carmen was very happy to hear the news. He had been taking care of the girl's children while they were recuperating. Carmen wanted to make sure that nothing else was going to happen to any of his family members. Carmen told Rudolpho that when he had a chance he wanted to talk to him about something important. He told Rudolpho to please come and see him at his home. Rudolpho told Carmen he would.

Later, Rudolpho came back to visit Carmen, as he was curious about what he wanted to discuss with him. When Rudolpho arrived at Carmen's home, Carmen took him into the kitchen. Carmen told Philomena that he had to talk over some business with Rudolpho and would she please give them some time alone.

This upset Philomena because she wanted to be involved in Carmen's business. Being the dutiful wife that she was though, Philomena told Carmen she had some work to do in her garden anyway. She told Carmen if he needed her she would be out there.

Philomena loved her garden. She had many rose bushes that had been there for some time. She took extremely good care of them. They were her pride and joy and she wanted to make sure they stayed beautiful all season.

Meanwhile, Carmen wanted to talk to Rudolpho in private. Once they were alone Carmen laid out his offer to Rudolpho. He wanted him to take over his business in East Baltimore. Carmen told Rudolpho that he wanted to retire and buy a nice home in Essex near the water. He wanted to be able to go fishing and boating. He just wanted to be able to relax and not worry about his gambling operation anymore. He was getting older and he wanted to enjoy his old age by doing the things he liked to do. He told Rudolpho that he didn't want to have to worry about people like Donald ever again. He was tired of dealing with these people who kept bugging him about things that he knew were not true.

Rudolpho told Carmen he would have to get back to him about the offer because this would be a huge responsibility for him to undertake. Rudolpho left Carmen's home to consider the offer he gave him.

Now Rudolpho was in a huge predicament. Alberto and Joseph, the bookies from Little Italy, had also made him a similar offer. He needed some time to think about this. He was really torn between these two offers. He had known Carmen for such a long time…he was beside himself.

Rudolpho decided to go and talk to his sister Michelle. Hopefully she would help him to decide what to do. Michelle had a way about her that made every situation come out in a light-hearted way. She never had a dumb or glum attitude. She was always upbeat and this is the reason he came to her with his problem. After he saw it in her eyes, she would always make the situation look bright.

When he went to talk to Michelle and tell her his situation, she responded to him, "You have known Carmen for many years and I know you are closer to him than you are with the Little Italy bookies. This should be a very easy decision for you to make now."

Michelle told Rudolpho, "If I were you, I would stay with Carmen." She also told him, "Carmen has never done you wrong has he?" Rudolpho told Michelle, "No, he has always treated me great."

Michelle said, "Well that should tell you what to do. Stay with Carmen."

With the advice that Michelle gave him, he knew what he had to do now.

After Rudolpho talked to his sister Michelle, he came back to talk to Carmen. Rudolpho was torn between the offers the Little Italy bookies gave him. They wanted him to run their operations in different parts of Baltimore. They were going to give him the full reigns of the control of these other parts of Baltimore.

Even after this offer Rudolpho felt Carmen and he had the same values. Carmen relied on Rudolpho to take care of a lot of his business. Carmen trusted Rudolpho tremendously. He never thought Rudolpho would do anything to betray him. Rudolpho thought he owed Carmen some loyalty because of all the things that Carmen did for him. When Rudolpho was a young boy, Carmen went to bat for him many times when he got in trouble. Rudolpho had broken into a store in the neighborhood with some of his young friends. All they wanted was to have some beer to drink. Rudolpho and his young friends were just out to have a good time. They did not think of the consequences if they got caught. But he did get caught.

Carmen put up the money for the lawyer to get him off of these charges. Rudolpho was always getting into scrapes when he was young. Carmen would always bail him out. Carmen knew Rudolpho's parents very well, as they all lived in the same neighborhood of East Baltimore. Carmen didn't want Rudolpho's Mom and Dad to be put through all the trouble of bailing Rudolpho out of jail. Carmen knew his parents didn't have much money. Rudolpho's dad worked hard at Bethlehem Steel. He had other children to support along with his wife. His wife stayed home and took care of the children and their home. Rudolpho never forgot what Carmen did for him.

This is the reason why Rudolpho wanted to stay loyal to Carmen. Rudolpho and Carmen had similar backgrounds. They both grew up in the same neighborhood. They worked hand and hand on many different things mainly with Carmen's bookie operation in East Baltimore. Rudolpho was Carmen's "go to man", and he depended on him for everything. Carmen believed that Rudolpho would never do anything to betray him. Rudolpho knew he was trusted by Carmen and he hoped that Carmen would never find out that the Little Italy bookies were also giving him money to do side jobs for them. It was unbelievable that Carmen's man, Rudolpho, could find out who was hurting the women before the police did.

CHAPTER SIXTEEN
Carmen's Relatives

The girls had been through a lot with their husbands. Their husbands became drug addicts. Giovanni, Nancy's husband kept hanging with people who were dealing drugs. He soon became a victim to the drugs they were selling and developed a full blown addiction. Unfortunately, it happened just before their child was born. Because of the addiction, Giovanni turned into a raging maniac within months. Nancy's husband beat her constantly if she didn't give him money to buy his drugs. Nancy didn't know what was happening. How could someone who was so loving, turn on her this way? They used to get along so good together and after he started to hang around with these certain people, he changed. These people were supposed to be Giovanni's friends but indeed they weren't. They introduced him to heroin. They enticed him into believing that this drug would make him feel so good.

They were only using Giovanni to get money out of his relative, Carmen. His so-called friends knew his relative had money. They thought if they got him involved with drugs, it would be easy for Giovanni to get money from Carmen. This method of theirs backfired on them because Carmen disliked drugs very much.

The nephews were draining their uncle of his money. Del Judajea tried to help his nephews out, but they were hooked on heroin. This is the drug that consumes your every being. Once you get involved with heroin, you cannot get off of it. The drug is supposed to be so great that your body wants more and more of it every day. If you don't get the drug your veins ache.

The boys continued to steal from the Del Judajeas so much that they disowned them from their family circle. The Del Judajeas barred them from their home. They did not want to be associated with drug activity. Del Judajea went against his blood relatives. Instead he protected the nephew's wives. He refused to give money to his nephews for drugs anymore. Carmen saw how his nephews got hooked on heroin, and he was determined to not have anything to do with this awful drug. Carmen only wanted to stick with the numbers racket, horse racing, football, basketball, and baseball games.

In the meantime, the bookies from Little Italy were thinking of extending their territory to different parts of Baltimore. They wanted to move their operation over to Hampden. They saw all the new bars and restaurants that were opening up in the area. They also took notice of how many young people were living in this area. They considered this area to be a good place for them to expand their operation.

Carmen, on the other hand, liked his comfort zone. He had the whole East side of Baltimore and he kept moving farther East more and more every week. He liked the idea of living near the water. He had intended to move there when he retired from his operation. But at the present time, he had no one to turn his operation over to, since his nephews were heavily involved with drugs. He made an offer to Rudolpho and he was waiting for his response.

The bookies, Alberto and Joseph, really didn't want to get involved with drugs either. The bookies from Little Italy had someone in a higher up position who was insisting for them to get involved in drugs. The certain person was one of the most prominent business men in Baltimore. The man owned the biggest tire distributing company on the East Coast. Their main man kept telling them they had to sell drugs. He told them there was a lot of money in drugs. This person was the Little Italy bookies main source, that had been fronting them money all of this time. So with their benefactors advice, Alberto and Joseph from Little Italy, decided to sell drugs. The man was considered to be a well known figure in Baltimore and because of their benefactor's prestige, they believed he knew what he was talking about.

Once, when Alberto and Joseph were at a restaurant in Little Italy, they saw the Del Judajeas. The Del Judajeas went to their favorite restaurant in Little Italy and saw Alberto and Joseph. They came over to the Del Judajea's table to talk to them. Alberto and Joseph told them about their plans to start selling drugs. Alberto and Joseph told them there was more money in drugs. They wanted the Del Judajeas to join them in this new adventure. The Del Judajeas told them it was not going to happen. Carmen told Alberto and Joseph, "Look what happened to my relatives. They are so strung out on heroin. Look what I have to do now. I have to take care of their wives and children because they are sick with the drugs." Carmen told them he didn't want anything to do with drugs.

Carmen told the bookies from Little Italy that the numbers racket was enough for him to deal with. He told them he was getting old and he wanted to retire in a few years. He didn't want to start on a new business adventure. He told them this was something he knew nothing about. Drugs were destructive and he didn't want to have anything to do with them.

When Alberto and Joseph heard this they became upset with Carmen. Alberto and Joseph told Carmen they were determined to sell drugs anyway. Little did Carmen know that Alberto and

Joseph were being influenced by their silent partner. Their main man was supplying the Little Italy bookies for some time. He was their money man. That was the reason why Alberto and Joseph wanted to sell drugs. Their benefactor kept insisting for them to do this. After the conversation that Alberto and Joseph had with Carmen they disengaged activities with him. The feud between the two bookies escalated.

One of the main reasons the Del Judajeas didn't want anything to do with drugs was because now the drug dealers were mixing fentanyl with heroin. It was bad enough for the addicts to put heroin in their veins. If a bubble happened in the tube, they would have a reaction from this, or possibly even die. When people added fentanyl to this mixture it had a more deadly affect on the people using it.

CHAPTER SEVENTEEN
The Bookies Meet in Little Italy

Carmen had some of his dealings in Little Italy because he frequented the restaurants there with his wife. When the Del Judajeas went to the restaurants in Little Italy they met some very influential people. The Del Judajeas met judges, district attorneys and many, many lawyers. Carmen became friends with these special people that he met at the restaurants. He kept these friends close to him because he knew he might need them sometime in the future. He also engaged in other things discreetly with them. These special people placed bets with Carmen on football games, basketball games, and numbers. This was one of the reasons why they were such good friends. They knew they could depend on each other if they needed any help down the road of life.

While the Del Judajeas were at their favorite restaurant, they would have the restaurant's famous Bookmaker salad with homemade dressing and their fabulous garlic bread. They loved their garlic bread. When they had these two items together they were just perfect for them for lunch.

The Little Italy bookies, Alberto and Joseph, were at the restaurant on this same day. They came over to the Del Judajea's table to talk to them about their plans to start selling drugs. Carmen reminded them that he did not want to get involved with drugs. Carmen was friends with all the judges and district attorneys. He told Alberto and Joseph he had enough to deal with his racketeering business. He was getting older and he wanted to retire from his business soon.

There was a lawyer who frequented the restaurant and the Del Judajeas liked him a lot. As a result of meeting this man, they became friends. The man had a friendly demeanor and he was also a comedian. Along with all of his many other good qualities, he would start to sing at a moment's notice. The man loved to sing and the bookies liked to hear this man sing. The songs that he sang were all Frank Sinatra songs. The Del Judajeas loved all the songs Frank Sinatra sang. The lawyer's name was Pitty. The Del Judajeas became very friendly with Pitty. After Pitty gave Carmen his card, he thanked him and kept his card, even though Carmen had a good lawyer. Carmen thought, you never know when you might need a lawyer.

Another person who struck the interest of the Del Judajeas while they were in the restaurant was Kevin. Carmen liked Kevin because he was a sharp dresser. Kevin always dressed in the latest style in men's clothes. The one thing that Carmen liked was clothes. He always wanted to dress in style. Carmen believed if his clothes had style it would make him look more businesslike to his associates.

Carmen and Kevin soon became friends. Carmen asked Kevin if it would be possible for him to come to his shop. Carmen wanted to check out the clothes that Kevin had. A date and time was set for Carmen to come to his shop and look at some of his clothes.

Carmen visited Kevin's shop located on Park Avenue downtown. He was surprised at the large selection there. Kevin told Carmen he goes to New York and Italy to buy clothes for his store. When Carmen heard this he became more interested in the clothes that were there. Carmen checked out the collection at Kevin's store. Carmen left the store with a few new outfits to wear.

Another man who came into the restaurant frequently was Lancaster. He came to the restaurant often and always sat at the same table. The table is now known as the Lancaster table. The table is located on the mezzanine in a corner. This is a very private section in the restaurant. While the man was there he was able to take care of his business. Lancaster had a stroke and it affected one of his arms. After the stroke he had trouble cutting his food so the waitresses would always help him out. He appreciated their help and he always took good care of them for helping him.

One day after lunch, Lancaster came outside and saw a man named Al. Al was a local who was a bookie by day and a maitre d' at Sabatino's in the evening. Because of Al's many dealings with people from all over Baltimore, Al had many things in his trunk. He would give these special items to many of his friends. On this day, while Al had his trunk open, he was looking for something special for one of his friends. When Lancaster saw Al, he came over and started talking to him. Lancaster told Al, "Al, you know what? My arm would go straight the day you pay me off." Of course, he was teasing Al, because this meant Al was bad pay.

Al was a very controversial person. He had many friends. He was friends with the Orioles baseball team. He was also friends with the players, coaches, and umpires from all the other teams. Because Al treated all of them so good, every time they came to Baltimore they would come into Sabatino's. When the players from the other teams, the managers and umpires came into Sabatino's and tasted their food, they were hooked. Every time the other team members, coaches, and umpires came back to Baltimore they always came into the restaurant to dine.

One evening when Al was driving home from the restaurant, he was swerving while he was driving up Pulaski Highway to go to his home in Rosedale. The police pulled him over because of the way he was driving. Al became so upset because of this, he thought they pulled him over because they knew he was a book-maker. He started yelling at the police and he told them, "I know you pulled me over because I'm a bookmaker."

After he said this to the police they made him open his trunk. In his trunk he had all the tickets for betting on football games and other gambling items. When they saw all these items they locked him up. If he hadn't said anything to them, they would have just given him a ticket for driving drunk.

The restaurant was also frequented by many bookies. They would frequently conduct some of their business while they were in the restaurant. One evening two bookies were trying to conduct some of their business in the restaurant. They had acquired a large amount of food stamps illegally. They were bragging about what they had to their friends. They tried to give them away to some of their friends. Of course one of the bookies was speaking a little louder than he should have. The bookie told his friend, "I can get you as many food stamps as you need."

At the table next to them were seated two detectives. They were dressed in plain clothes so no one knew who they were. The bookies had no idea who they were either, but that didn't seem to bother them. They just continued to boast about what they could do for their friends. While they were talking to their friends about the food stamps the two detectives were listening to everything they were saying. The bookies were trying to cut a deal right there in the restaurant. After the bookies completed their deal, the two detectives got up from their seats and arrested everyone involved right there in the restaurant.

Because the bookies from Little Italy were looking to branch their operation out, the only thing they needed was someone to do this for them. As soon as Donald recovered from his injuries, he went to talk to the Little Italy bookies. He told them he would like to work for them because he was done with the Del Judajeas. He told the bookies from Little Italy that the Del Judajeas were bad pay. He told them this was the reason why he didn't want to have anything more to do with them. When in reality, it was because Donald had gotten beaten up by Rudolpho's men. He needed a job he was very low on cash. After the conversation that Donald had with the bookies from Little Italy, Donald became their "go to man".

The Little Italy bookies really wanted Rudolpho to take over this job. Rudolpho had more of a level head than Donald did. Rudolpho was able to take control of any crisis in a more professional way. Rudolpho had not gotten back to the Little Italy bookies about their offer. Rudolpho left the Little Italy bookies unsure if he was going to work for them. Alberto and Joseph accepted Donald's proposal to work for them.

CHAPTER EIGHTEEN
The Jealousy

The bookies from Little Italy were looking to branch out their operation to different parts of Baltimore. With all the restaurants and trendy places that were opening in the Hampden area, it became more appealing to the bookies from Little Italy. Alberto and Joseph wanted to have one of their people work this area for them.

One day Carmen ran into Alberto at the barber shop. They both went to the same barber because they always wanted to look good for their public. Their barber's name was Freddie. He always took good care of the bookies because they were regular customers. All of them – Carmen, Alberto, and Freddie were Italian and because of this they became friends. While they were there for some time they finally started to speak to each other. Alberto was the first person to strike up a conversation with Carmen. Alberto could not resist what he was going to say to Carmen.

Alberto said, "I see you have Rudolpho working for you full time now,"

Carmen said, "Yes, he is working for me full time."

Alberto said to Carmen, "Did you know Rudolpho had been working for us for some time?"

Carmen replied, "Oh really? How long did he work for you guys?"

Alberto replied, "He worked for us for several years."

Carmen didn't say anything else. He just sat in the barber shop and made out that he was reading a magazine. In the meantime he was fuming inside.

As soon as Carmen came home he called Rudolpho. He asked him to come over to his home. Rudolpho arrived at Carmen's home and he walked in not knowing what he was going to be hit with. Carmen told Rudolpho to come into the kitchen... he had something he wanted to talk to him about. Carmen asked Philomena to please go outside and attend to her flower garden. Carmen told her he had something important to talk to Rudolpho about.

With Carmen's suggestion Philomena went into her garden. Carmen immediately started to question Rudolpho.

Carmen asked Rudolpho, "When were you going to tell me you had been working for Alberto and Joseph?"

Rudolpho didn't know what to say at first. He was blindsided. Rudolpho said, "Yes I worked for them but I never discussed your business with them." Rudolpho added, "I have been loyal to you always. I would never betray you after all of the things you have done for me and my family."

Rudolpho asked Carmen to please forgive him for not telling him about Alberto and Joseph.

Rudolpho told Carmen, "I would never do for them what I do for you. I really care about you Carmen. I would not do anything to hurt you."

Carmen was still upset so he told Rudolpho to leave. He had to think about this situation for a while.

Alberto told Carmen about Rudolpho because the Little Italy bookies really wanted Rudolpho to work for them. Alberto was upset that Rudolpho wouldn't handle their businesses. He was jealous of Carmen. Alberto and Joseph knew Rudolpho had a level head. When Rudolpho didn't reply, they had no idea who they were going to get to work these different areas for them.

Donald came to Alberto and Joseph and told them he could work for them if they wanted him to. Even though they knew Donald for some time they still liked Rudolpho better. As Alberto and Joseph took Donald's offer into consideration, they didn't know of anyone else who could handle their bookie operations.

This is how Donald got to handle the Little Italy bookies operations. Alberto and Joseph wanted to branch out. They had a lot of ambition. They knew there were other parts of Baltimore that had many people who wanted to place bets on football and basketball games. They also knew that there were many people who wanted to play the numbers every day.

Carmen barely had time to clear his head about everything that had been going on in his and Philomena's life, but he kept his confidence in Rudolpho. He believed everything that Rudolpho told him. So he kept the offer he proposed to Rudolpho about taking over his business. As a result of what happened to Philomena, he wanted to end his business. Carmen wanted to move to Essex and buy a home near the water. He wanted to be able to relax and enjoy the rest of his life with his wonderful wife Philomena.

He was going to let his relatives have his home. There were three women, but Carmen wanted to let the women decide who would get the home. It was large enough at least for two families to live there. Carmen did not think that the women would argue over who was going to have his home. He believed whoever was able to use his home would enjoy it. The children went to school in the area, so this would be good for all of them. They wouldn't have to go far to go to school. Carmen was going to leave everything up to the women. They could decide among themselves what to do with his offer.

CHAPTER NINETEEN
Setting up Shop in Hampden

Hampden is a 19th century neighborhood. There are houses there that were built in the 1880's that are still there today. Hampden is a little island. There are a lot of businesses located in Hampden. Johns Hopkins University is one of the most prominent places located in the neighborhood.

North of Hampden is Roland Park, the part of town where many elaborate homes are located. West of Hampden is the Jones Falls Expressway. Up and down the Jones Falls there is a huge section of stone and brick warehouses.

A manufacturing plant that makes canvas for all the big ships is located there. One of the older buildings in Hampden is where the police horses were kept back in the day.

Years ago, many mills were located in Hampden. People who lived there during this time all worked in the mills. Today, most of the old mills are transformed into condominiums where many young people live. Many office buildings are now located where the old mills used to be.

Most of the people who live in Hampden have lived there for some time. These people are part of the fixture of the neighborhood. Now there are many young people who live there also. The young people who moved there are married and are building families.

There is a street in Hampden that is decorated every year at Christmas time. This street is 34th Street. The people who live on this street string Christmas lights from house to house and across the street. It is a beautiful sight to behold at Christmas time. The people who live on this street welcome hundreds of strangers constantly during the Christmas season. There is a man who lives on this block that makes a Christmas tree out of hub caps and displays it in front of his home. On New Year's Eve there is a huge celebration on the street.

Another very famous street located in Hampden is 36th Street, more commonly known as "the Avenue" by the locals. This street also has many restaurants on it. One of them is The Café Hon Restaurant. On 36th Street there are the names of the two people who fought in wars and lived in the Hampden area then. One of the men fought in the Civil War and the other man fought in World War II. They are Lt. Richetts, US Navy, and Pvt. Sheriden who was in the US Army. There is also a monument on Cheswick Road in Hampden that honors the First World War Victims. There is also a World War II monument for all the people who lost their lives.

36th Street is famous for many specialty shops, book stores, and many other restaurants. There are also many shops that sell

vintage articles. A famous book store that is on 36th Street is called The Ivy book store. John Waters had a book signing there once and people were lined up out onto the street to have their book signed by him. All the authors that come there are able to talk about their books. He also had a book signing at the Atomic book store.

During the summer months, there is a huge festival held on 36th Street called the Hon Festival. All the shops put their items outside. There is a band stand where local people perform. People dress up like they did back in the 50's. Women piled their hair high upon their head. The Mayor always has the Christmas Parade there.

On top of the hill on 41st Street is where all the local TV stations are located. There is a huge transmitter located on top of the hill for Channels 11, 13 and 45.

A local man, named Manny, living in Hampden is considered to be the watch dog of the area. Manny is very tall and has gray hair and a gray beard. He always surveys the area. On one occasion, while he was walking his grandson, he noticed a tall man walking around the neighborhood. He had never seen him before and the man looked like he didn't know where he was going.

Manny, being the most inquisitive person, went over to the man and asked him if he needed any help. The man told Manny he was fine. He told Manny he was going to move into the area and he just wanted to check it out. After Donald told Manny this he left him alone.

In reality, Donald was looking for a place to move to so he could set up his operation for the Little Italy bookies. His bosses believed they could easily get their other agendas started there also. The bookies believed that people who lived in this area were looking for someone to place bets with on the games. They were right. The young people were looking for a way to do this because they were interested in the different sports events going on. They wanted to try their luck but had no one to do this with.

Donald started checking out some of the places in the neighborhood. He became friendly with the bartenders that he met in the bars. He talked to many bartenders asking them if they knew of any people who might want to place bets on the games. Donald told the bartenders if they would get him some action there would be something in it for them. With this the bartenders agreed to ask some of their regular customers about this.

The bartenders told Donald they already knew of some people who would be interested in betting on the games. When Donald left the bar he left a big tip for the bartenders so they would remember him. He also gave the bartender his cell phone number so they would be able to get in touch with him.

As soon as the bartender's regular customers came into the restaurant the bartenders told them they wanted to talk to them about something. The bartenders told their customers that they knew of a person who would be able to take their bets. The bartenders told the customers the bookie pays better than the regular lottery does. As a result of the bartenders putting this information out there, they began to get some customers for their new friend Donald.

Donald surveyed the area and settled on the restaurant called The Rocket to Venus. The Rocket to Venus was frequented by many young people. These are the people that Donald wanted to talk to. He knew that most of them would like to place wagers on the different games.

The Rocket to Venus got its name from a man who wanted to send a rocket to Venus. The man's name was Robert Condit and he was a recent graduate from Poly High School. Robert got his ambition to go to Venus while listening to the news of how Lindberg had flown over the Atlantic Ocean. When Robert heard about Lindberg it fueled his enthusiasm to go to Venus.

Robert had the idea to visit Venus for some time. Robert, his brother Harry, and a friend Sterling, built a space ship. They didn't plan for anything that would happen after they got there. They didn't know if there would be food or water there or not. They figured that once they landed there, they would find all this out.

Robert and his friends didn't take any food with them. They only took water. They didn't know what to expect once they got there. Robert figured after they got there, if there was no food or water there, they would just come back to earth and get some food. Of course he did not plan on how they would be able to get back to earth after they landed on Venus. Robert did not have any foresight on what to do once they got there either.

As soon as the rocket was built, Robert and his friends tried to start the rocket up. There was so much smoke and flames and a huge fire. The fire department had to be called to put the fire out. Robert tried to light the rocket up again but after he did this the rocket still wouldn't take off. He finally realized the rocket would not be able to take off without a booster rocket. Robert knew they did not have enough money to build this so that was the end of their excursion to Venus. He also did not know what the temperature was on the planet. Was it cold or hot there? Robert did not plan what would happen once they got there either. After he encountered all these obstacles, this was the end of his huge plans to go to Venus. A replica of the rocket is now located on top of the building of the restaurant which is called The Rocket to Venus.

Most of the restaurants in Hampden have TV's in them. The owners of the restaurants know that people always want to know what the score of the game is. Therefore the people can dine and watch the sports games on TV while they are in the restaurants. The young people were looking for somewhere or someone they could place a wager with. Donald believed with all the activity from all the young people who went to this location, it would be a perfect spot to set up his gambling operation.

Donald became a regular customer at the Rocket to Venus. The bartenders got to know him by his name and made sure that they had his drink ready for him when he came in. The bartender's names were Colin and Alex.

Donald asked them, "Do some of your customers ever ask you if you know anyone they could place a bet with?"

The bartenders told Donald that the customers asked this question all the time. Donald asked the bartenders if they would be able to find some customers for him. Donald told them they would be given a piece of the action. The bartenders told Donald there were many enthusiastic people who were interested in sports. Colin and Alex told Donald that the customers were anxious to place some wagers on the games. Donald replied that this was perfect. Soon the action was set up for their little operation. Now Donald had a couple places set up in Hampden!

Donald went back to his friends in Little Italy and told them he had some connections in Hampden. They were pleased with this information because they wanted to branch their operation out in different areas in Baltimore. Now that Donald had his operations set up in Hampden, he stopped sending letters to Philomena. He had other interests and he didn't want to worry about the Del Judajeas anymore.

CHAPTER TWENTY
Life Goes On

Ed and Rosie had been spending so much time working on this case that they hardly had any time to be with their families. The two detectives made up their minds that nothing was going to take them away from their families this weekend, no matter what came up. They needed it for themselves, and their children needed it too.

Rosie planned to have a cookout for her children, Rachel and Tyler, and her husband Bernie. She went to the market and bought corn on the cob, chicken, hot dogs, and ground beef to make hamburgers. Rosie decided that nothing was going to interrupt her plans to make this weekend special for her family. She had been working day and night on this case. It seemed that every time she wanted to do something with her family another thing came up about the case. When something came up about the case she and Ed would have to trace the lead that had come up. Therefore her family would be put on hold once again. Rosie thought this was going to be her family's weekend and she would make sure of it.

She and her husband Bernie hadn't had any quality time together either. Rosie was going to change that this weekend also. This was going to be their children's time to have their mother and father with them playing games, eating and just having some good fun together. Bernie was off from the Sun Paper this weekend also. Everything was set for the whole family to be together.

Ed wanted to be with Helen also. He missed her terribly. Just being able to hold her in his arms would be fine with him. Ed called Helen to find out if this weekend would be okay for them to get together. Helen was so glad to hear from Ed. She understood that his job was confining but she didn't think it would take him away from her for such a long time. Helen made up her mind that she was going to have a serious talk with Ed when she saw him again. While Rosie's weekend was playing out the way she wanted it to, Ed was also planning to spend some quality time with Helen.

Helen told Ed she couldn't understand why he wasn't able to spend more time with her during the week. Ed told Helen it was hard for him to be with her during the week because of their conflicting work hours. Ed told Helen that by the time he was finishing up his reports, she would probably be sleeping. Helen told Ed he could call her anyway. It didn't matter what time it was. Helen told Ed it would be so good just to hear from him during the middle of the week.

Ed said he didn't want to keep her up late because he knew she had to get up early in the morning. He told Helen he didn't want anything to happen to her. Helen said she would like to know if he was okay and how his case was progressing. Helen told Ed she worried about him when she didn't hear from him. She told Ed that it would be wonderful to hear from him in the evening before she went to bed. Ed told Helen he thought he would be bothering her and he didn't want to do that. Helen told Ed that he would not be a bother to her. It would be a delight. After Ed heard this he agreed to call Helen during the middle of the week to let her know how everything was doing. He also wanted to know how she was doing. They both missed each other so. If he called her during the week he could keep her informed about how his case was coming along. Ed told Helen how very much he missed being with her. He told Helen he would love to hold her in his arms and kiss her goodnight every night.

Next Ed asked her what was she doing this weekend, and if he could see her. Helen told Ed that would be so nice. As a result of their conversation their date was set for this weekend. Helen suggested to Ed, instead of his taking her out to dinner why didn't she cook a dinner for him at her home? Ed told Helen that would be just wonderful. He hadn't had a home cooked meal for some time.

Ed told Helen his sister Paula would occasionally bring him her famous eggplant Parmesan. Since her daughter had a baby it was hard for her to do this for him now.

Ed told Helen he would bring a couple of bottles of wine. He asked her what kind would she like. Helen told him that she really liked Merlot. As soon as the date and time were set for them to see each other again, they could not wait for their date to begin.

Meanwhile Rosie and Bernie took the children to see an Orioles game on this weekend. The Orioles were on a winning streak, and they won the game, which was fabulous. This made their time at the game more exciting. They all had a wonderful time cheering for the Orioles at the ballpark. The children couldn't wait for the next day so they could have their big cookout. This was going to be a wonderful time for all of them. They were able to have both of their parents with them the whole weekend. As soon as they came home from the ballpark, the children went to bed. They wanted to make sure they would be able to get up early the next day to have their cookout.

Rosie and Bernie were just fine with that because then the two of them could have some special time together. This was something Bernie and Rosie wanted to happen for some time. When Bernie took Rosie in his arms she felt that wonderful feeling that she got every time she was with Bernie. They were in each other's arms once again and it was good just being together.

Rosie told Bernie how very much she missed being held in his arms. She loved him so. Bernie told Rosie he missed having their special time together. Bernie told Rosie she worked too many hours. Once Bernie took Rosie in his arms their lovely evening began. He didn't want this evening to stop. It was a wonderful feeling being together. Rosie told Bernie they had to do this more often.

Ed arrived at Helen's home with wine and roses. Helen was so excited to see the roses and Ed, she gave him a big hug and kiss on his cheek. Ed took Helen in his arms and told her how very much he missed her. He gave her a warm and tender kiss. Ed and Helen were so happy to be together after all the days of their being apart. It was simply wonderful being in each other's arms.

Ed told Helen he cared very much for her and he wanted to spend more time with her. He didn't know how he was going to be able to do this with the way he had to work. Helen told Ed, "Maybe we can work something out."

The wine Ed brought was Helen's favorite Merlot. It went well with the dinner Helen had prepared for Ed. Helen made her family's recipe of homemade sauce and meatballs. They had spaghetti and meatballs and salad. The dinner was fabulous. Ed told Helen she was a great cook. As soon as the dinner was over Helen told Ed she wanted to talk to him about something important. Ed became a little upset because he had no idea what Helen was going to say.

Helen and Ed went in the living room to sit and talk about their future. Ed told Helen he wanted to explain his job to her. He began the conversation with when he first entered the police force. He told Helen when he was a rookie he thought being on the murder squad was the best thing ever. He told Helen he looked up to the guys who were on this particular squad. He told her he took all the harassments because he wanted to be on the homicide squad. He believed if he got on this squad he could do a good job.

At this time though he told her that he was becoming more agitated than ever with his job. He thought that it was because of the long hours. He told Helen maybe it was because he was not able to be with her. Ed told Helen he was trying to control his temper before the job took hold of him.

Helen asked Ed what he would think about moving in with her. This was the special thing that Helen wanted to talk to Ed about. Ed asked Helen to be sure she wanted this. Helen told him she did. Helen told Ed she had been considering asking him this for some time, only she didn't know how he would react. Then Helen said to Ed, "What do you think about my idea?"

Ed told Helen he didn't want to impose on her because of the different hours that they worked. Ed told her if she really didn't mind his crazy hours he would love to live with her.

Ed told Helen, "That way we could be together all the time," Ed said, "Do you think I would be cramping your style?"

Helen replied to Ed, "If I thought you would be doing this, I never would have asked you to move in the first place."

Ed grabbed her hand and kissed it and then Helen moved closer to Ed. They spent the rest of the evening in each other's arms. It was a fabulous evening together once more.

Ed was so happy that Helen felt the same way about him as he did about her. They were both busy with their lives but this did not stop them from caring about each other. Later that evening Ed told Helen he wanted to be with her always. This was the beginning of a wonderful life together for them.

The next morning Helen made breakfast for them. Then they spent the rest of Sunday afternoon together in each other's arms. Ed told Helen he would start to pack his things and ask his brother-in-law Chuck if he would be able to help him move.

CHAPTER TWENTY-ONE
The Investigation Resumes

The next morning, after Rosie and Ed had their wonderful weekend with their loved ones, they received a call from Anna, the Captain's secretary. Anna told the detectives the Captain wanted the two detectives to go to the hospital and question the two women. Anna told them they were being released from the hospital today. The two detectives went to bring the two women, Glenda and Patricia, in for questioning. They picked up Nancy and brought her in for questioning also. They put all of them in separate rooms so they could interrogate them alone. They didn't want any of them to find out what the other women were saying. The detectives knew that if the women were together, they could compare notes. Then their stories would all be the same.

While the women were in different interview rooms the detectives took their time questioning them. They did this because they were trying to make the women nervous. But in another way they wanted to make them calm so they would not be afraid to talk to them. The detectives knew if they didn't have the women relaxed they wouldn't be able to get good responses from them. Later when the detectives had the witnesses calm, they might be able to catch them in a lie.

When the detectives finally went back to talk to the women they were all upset. The women wanted to get back to their children and their homes. They hadn't been with them for some time and they missed them terribly. The detectives had a reason for doing this. They figured by now they would be willing to talk. They were right.

Nancy was the first victim so she was the person that they questioned first. The two detectives started right in with questions, not giving her time to think. They asked her, "Why do you think this man wanted to hurt you?" Nancy told them she did not know the man. She had never seen this man before.

Next they asked her, "What are you telling us? You're telling us you never saw this person at the strip club where you worked at before? Are you sure you never saw him in the club?" Nancy had to think for a while before she gave them her answer. Nancy told the detectives the club was dark and she could not say if he was in there or not. She told the detectives she didn't remember seeing him in the club. Nancy told the detectives there were many regular customers that came into the club.

The detectives said to Nancy, "Well, there must have been some reason why this person was hurting you." Nancy kept insisting she had no idea why he did this to her. She did not know him.

"Okay then," the detectives said, "Tell us about your husband. Did your husband know this man?" Nancy told the detectives she didn't know if her husband Giovanni knew this man or not. Nancy told the detectives she hadn't been with her husband for some time. Therefore she could not tell the detectives if her husband knew this man.

The detectives replied, "There had to be some reason why he hurt you." Nancy told them the man wanted to know where her in-laws kept their money. Nancy said she kept telling the man she did not know where they kept their money. The detectives

THE BALTIMORE BOOKIES

repeated, "Well, there had to be some reason why he singled you out." Nancy told the detectives, "Maybe the man came after us because our husbands were their nephews."

After getting this statement from Nancy, they left her in the investigating room alone. They wanted her to wonder why they were keeping her there. They went to the other investigating room to question Glenda. Glenda wanted to know why she was brought in for questioning. The detectives told her they wanted to ask her what she thought the reason was that this man attacked her. She told the detectives she had no idea. She told the detectives she had never seen this man before this incident.

The detectives asked her, "Do you mean you never saw him in the restaurant where you worked?" Glenda told the detectives while she was at work she was busy serving the customers.

The detectives asked her again, "Do you mean to tell us that you did not know this man or his reason for attacking you?"

Glenda said, "That is exactly what I am telling you."

Next, the detectives asked her, "Was your assailant coming after you to get to your husband?" Glenda told the detectives she hadn't been with her husband, Vincenso, for some time. She told the detectives the man kept asking her where her in-laws kept their money. Glenda kept telling the man she had no idea where they kept their money.

Since the detectives kept getting the same answer from Glenda as they did from Nancy, they left her alone in the interrogating room. The detectives wanted Glenda to think about what they had asked her. Again, the detectives did not get any information out of Glenda, so they went to question the third woman, Patricia.

The detectives went to the interrogating room that Patricia was in. They asked her the same question that they asked the

Page 132

other two women. And Patricia gave the detectives the same answer as Nancy and Glenda gave them. The detectives wanted to know what she was doing in Fort McHenry.

Patricia told the detectives she had gone out with some of her friends in south Baltimore. She told the detectives this man was in the same club that she was in. She told the detectives this man came over to her and started talking to her. She said when he started to talk to her he seemed very nice. The man bought all the girls a drink. After he did this they all thought the man was a good person. While they were talking the man asked her if she would like to get something to eat. He told her he would take her to someplace nice, and then he said to her, "Let's get out of here." Because Patricia believed the man was nice she decided to leave with him. She told her friends good bye, and they seemed to be okay with this. They all believed the man was a nice person.

After she got in his car, he started to question her about her in-laws. She knew right then and there she had made a big mistake. She told him she didn't know anything about her relative's personal life. As soon as she said this to him he became belligerent and started threatening her. He took her to a secluded place and beat her. As he was hurting her he kept telling her that she knew where they kept their money. He kept saying, "Tell me. Come on and tell me where the Del Judajeas keep their money." She told the detectives, that when she didn't tell him where they kept the money, he kept hitting her. She said after that she didn't remember anything because she passed out. With this answer, the detectives left her alone and went to talk among themselves.

After many hours of interrogating the three women, the detectives finally had something to go on. The detectives had wanted to see if they could make the women break. It finally worked. The women opened up and told the detectives that their relatives were the biggest book makers in East Baltimore. They told the detectives that the man was trying to go through them to get to the Del Judajeas. It didn't work, though. They wouldn't budge. They were trying to protect the Del Judajeas. They told the detectives they didn't realize it would amount to all of this.

Their assailant thought, if he hurt them, he could get the money from the bookie. When they wouldn't help him, he became angry with them. This was the reason why he beat them. The women were afraid to talk because the man told them if they went to the police he was going to hurt their children. Because of this they kept quiet. Glenda was the person who finally gave in to the detectives. She was afraid for her children, but she knew she had to talk to the detectives.

After all of the months of the police investigating this matter, they finally got the women to tell them what they wanted. The women told the detectives the Del Judajeas were the biggest bookies in East Baltimore. As soon as the detectives got this information from the women their next move was to go and talk to Captain Dave. When they got into his office they told him what the women told them. They asked Captain Dave "Is it okay now to bring the Del Judajeas in for questioning?" Captain Dave told the detectives, "Yes, bring Carmen in for questioning." That was exactly what the detectives did.

CHAPTER TWENTY-TWO
The Questioning

As soon as the detectives found out what the women who were injured told them, they definitely wanted to talk to the Del Judajeas. The detectives, Ed and Rosie, went back to the Del Judajea's home to bring them in for questioning.

The detectives put them in separate rooms. They wanted to interrogate them individually. They had the information from the women. Now all the detectives had to do was to get statements from the Del Judajeas. They also had the information from Ed's friend Fast Eddie about all the activity that was coming and going in their home.

Carmen Del Judajea was not ready for the detectives today. They surprised him when they came back to his home and took him and his wife in for questioning. First, they went into the room that Carmen was in. The detectives entered the interview room carrying stacks of paper. They wanted to make Carmen think they had a lot of evidence on him, which they did. Ed kept going through the papers to make Carmen think he had something new on him.

Ed and Rosie took their time with him. They asked him if he wanted anything to drink or if he was hungry. Carmen replied that he was fine. It was obvious that he was upset that the detectives brought them in for questioning again. Carmen wanted to get the investigation over with so they could go home.

The detectives wanted to make him relax so he would be more cooperative.

This time, when they read Carmen his rights, they didn't want to mess anything up since they had the evidence against him. Carmen told them he was fine, he had a lawyer. He didn't need one from the court system. Next, Ed started the questioning.

"Okay Carmen, the girls told us you are the biggest bookie in Baltimore. Is this true?"

Carmen replied, "No, it is not true."

Ed said to Carmen, "This is what the women told us. Are you telling us they are not telling the truth?"

Carmen told the detectives, "Yes, I am telling you, this is not true."

Rosie said to Carmen, "I don't believe the women were lying to us."

Ed said, "Why is it not true? The girls told us the reason they were beaten was because of you."

Rosie told Carmen, "The man insisted that you owed him a lot of money. He wanted them to get it for him. The fact that the women wouldn't help him was the reason why he hurt them." Carmen wouldn't respond to their allegations.

Ed told Carmen, "Well, there had to be some reason for the man to hurt the women. The suspect knew that they were all related to you and this is why he singled them out. Carmen, are you still insisting that the women are not telling us the truth?"

Carmen wouldn't answer their questions. The women had told the detectives that the man was going to hurt their children if they went to the police about him.

Then Rosie got close to Carmen and told him, "The girls told us the perp was trying to go through them to get to you. He told them that you owe him a lot of money and he wanted it." Rosie continued, "Does this ring a bell with you? Do you owe this person a lot of money?"

Although Rosie asked him this question there still was no response from Carmen.

Then Ed got up and asked Carmen this question, "Were you taking book from him?" Finally, Carmen told Ed that he wasn't taking bets from Donald.

Ed then said to Carmen, "Well, why was he beating the women up to get to you? Did he have an alternative reason for doing this to them?"

Rosie got up and said, "Come on Carmen. The girls told us this and we believe them. They told us they were afraid for their children."

Ed added, "Does this mean anything to you? Are you a heartless person?"

Ed asked, "Do you want something to happen to those children? They are part of your blood aren't they? They are your nephew's children aren't they?"

Rosie said, "What do you think this person is going to do if you don't pay him? Don't you think he will keep his word?" Carmen still wouldn't answer her.

As a result of the detectives double-talking him, Carmen started to get nervous. They kept walking around the interview room while they were talking to him one at a time. They took their time while they were questioning him. They questioned him over and over again. They were trying to catch him in a lie. But Carmen would not budge. He kept saying, "No comment, no comment."

The detectives told Carmen they would keep what he told them to themselves. That was the oldest trick in the book. They told Carmen they didn't want to see anything happen to the children. Carmen still wouldn't budge.

The detectives told him, "We have the statements from your relatives. Each one of them told us the same thing over and over again."

Ed said to Carmen, "Why are you still insisting that this is not true?"

Rosie chimed in and asked Carmen, "Are you telling me the women are lying?"

Ed said, "Is this what you are telling us? The women are lying?"

The two detectives kept hitting Carmen with one question after another. They didn't want to give him a chance to think. They wanted him to answer their questions. They were trying to make him come up with the answers they wanted to hear. They were trying to get him to tell them his side of the story. They didn't want to lose him. They thought they had him thinking but he still wouldn't budge. He kept repeating, "No comment, no comment." He believed if he kept saying this, they would not be able to hold him.

They even told Carmen that they felt sorry for him, because they knew the trouble he had with his nephews.

The detectives told Carmen, "Now, we know the responsibility you took on because you and your wife are caring for the children of your nephews." The detectives told Carmen they knew he was doing a lot to protect the children.

The detectives became upset because they could not get a response from Carmen. Even with the evidence on him, they were going to have to try a different tactic to get Carmen to talk. They left him in the interrogating room by himself and went to question Philomena alone.

The detectives thought if they put the same questions to Philomena as they did to Carmen she would break and tell them the truth. They knew she did not want to see the children get hurt. She was a woman, and they knew she was the motherly type. They knew she would break if they kept questioning her the same way they questioned Carmen. This is exactly what they did.

First, they asked her if she needed a lawyer. After they asked her this, Philomena told the detectives she had a lawyer. She told the detectives it was their family lawyer whom they had for many years.

Then the detectives went at her with everything they had. They told Philomena that the women told them Carmen was a big bookie. They asked her, "Is this true, Philomena?" Philomena was afraid to talk. She didn't want to get her husband in any trouble. She just sat there at first, not saying anything. They could tell she was thinking very hard. Philomena became bewildered.

Rosie told Philomena, "The man told the women if he didn't get the money that Carmen owed him, he was going to hurt the children," Rosie continued, "Is this what you want?"

Ed chimed in, "Do you want to see the children being hurt?"

Rosie said, "Are you going to answer us?"

Ed said, "What is wrong with you Philomena?"

Rosie repeated, "Yes, do you want to see the children hurt?"

With all these questions being asked all at once, Philomena started to cry. She told the detectives she didn't know what to do. They told her, "You have to do the right thing. Don't you understand the children will be hurt? Is this what you want? Do you want to see the children hurt?"

The detectives kept grilling her over and over again until she finally broke. Philomena told the detectives that she believed that the man who was hurting the women must have been the same person that had been arguing with her husband a while ago. She told the detectives a weird man was harassing her husband. Philomena said the man insisted her husband owed him money.

She said, "The man said he would get his money one way or another." Philomena believed this was the reason he was hurting her family members.

She started to cry and sob. She was torn between her love for her husband and her love for the children. She was beside herself. She was so confused she really didn't know what to do. Finally after an hour of questioning and more crying, Philomena told the detectives she wanted to talk to her husband. She told them it was imperative. She needed to talk to Carmen.

Of course, they could not let her do this. They told her she had to answer their questions before she could talk to her husband. Philomena broke down and started to cry uncontrollably. This made the detectives very upset. They didn't want anything to happen to her.

They went to Captain Dave and told him that Carmen's wife was crying hysterically. What should they do? She wanted to talk to her husband and they had told her she couldn't talk to him until she told them what had happened. They asked the Captain again, "What should we do? We don't want anything to happen to her. She is an old person." The Captain told them to leave her alone for a while and see if she changed her story.

When the detectives came back to interview Philomena, she got herself together. And to their surprise the first thing out of Philomena's mouth was, "I want to talk to a lawyer." She told the detectives she wasn't going to talk to them anymore. She insisted that she wanted to talk to a lawyer. She told them she knew her rights. She wasn't as naive as the detectives thought. She just kept insisting that she wanted to talk to her lawyer. She told the detectives if they wouldn't let her talk to Carmen, she wanted to talk to her lawyer.

The detectives were in shock. They couldn't believe that Philomena had that much know-how about what to do in this situation. They had underestimated her. They should have known she knew something, because she was married to Carmen. Carmen must have told her a while back that if she were ever confronted by the police, to ask for a lawyer.

This was the end of the detectives questioning Philomena. They became upset because they couldn't get any information out of her. The detectives had no other choice but to get her a lawyer. After this they had to let her go.

The two detectives knew all the tactics to get someone to talk but that didn't work with Carmen or Philomena. They were two tough Italian people who had been around for some time and they weren't going to give in to the detectives. Even when the detectives told them that the children might be hurt they still wouldn't give in to them.

The detectives questioned both of them for over an hour each and they still wouldn't talk. The detectives tried to use every tactic that they knew but it didn't matter with the Del Judajeas. They did not budge. Things did not go the way the detectives had hoped they would go. This upset the two detectives tremendously. Even though they had the evidence to hold Carmen, they still couldn't get him to talk.

The one thing the detectives had in their favor was the statements from the three women. Because they had those statements, they were able to hold Carmen. Even though Carmen wouldn't budge, the extensive interview and the evidence was enough to hold him. The detectives told the police to take Carmen to a holding cell. The detectives had the information they needed to keep Carmen locked up.

CHAPTER TWENTY-THREE
Philomena and Carmen

As a result of the information the detectives received from the women, Carmen was detained at the police station. Philomena was released from the police. Even though the detectives offered to give her a ride home, Philomena refused to be driven home by the police. Philomena called her friend Rita, and asked her if it would be possible for her to come to the police station and take her home.

Philomena told Rita, "They are keeping my husband here at the police station for more questioning. I have to go home so I can try to get some help to get him out of here." Rita told Philomena she would be there to take her home as soon as possible. Rita also asked her if there were anything else she could do for her.

Philomena answered,, "I will fill you in on everything while you are driving me home."

Philomena had to wait at the police station for her friend Rita. While she was there, she became more and more upset. She couldn't believe that the women, whom they had been helping all of this time, went against Carmen. She couldn't believe the women told the detectives that Carmen was a big bookie. The more Philomena thought about this, the more upset she became. After all that she and Carmen had done for the women. It was unbelievable that the women could have turned against them.

By the time Rita arrived at the police station, Philomena was fuming. She couldn't wait to get home. She had a lot of business to take care of. On the way home Philomena told Rita that the women that they had been helping all this time had told the detectives that Carmen was the biggest bookie in East Baltimore. Rita couldn't believe all the things that Philomena was telling her. Rita knew that Philomena needed her help now more than ever before. Rita told Philomena that she would help her with whatever she needed through this awful ordeal.

As soon as Philomena got home, the first person she called was Carmen's friend Rudolpho. Philomena asked Rudolpho to come to her home. She needed to see him for moral support. Rudolpho could not believe what Philomena was telling him. He also could not believe that the women went against Carmen after all he had done for them.

While Carmen was in jail he was allowed one phone call. He called his lawyer and friend Joseph to come and get him out of jail. Carmen was so worried about Philomena. He knew how upset she got when things like this happened to them.

Joseph arrived at the police station. He tried to get Carmen released from jail. However, it seemed that there was a problem. The person who was in charge of letting Carmen go couldn't find the paperwork on him. This was because Carmen had just been locked up. Usually after a person is arrested it takes some time for the paper work to get to the proper people.

Joseph went to see Captain Dave. When Joseph entered the Captain's office he was greeted by Anna, the Captain's secretary. Joseph told Anna it was imperative for him to talk to the Captain. Anna went in the Captain's office and told him that a lawyer named Joseph was outside and he needed to talk to him. It was an emergency. The Captain told Anna, "Let him in. He is a friend of mine."

As soon as Joseph entered the Captain's office he confronted him with this issue. Joseph said to the Captain, "What is the problem here? I have come here to get my client out of jail and they can't find his paperwork," Joseph asked again, "What is the problem?" The Captain called his secretary to his office.

When Anna came into his office he told her to find out what was holding up the paperwork for Carmen to be released. Anna went looking for detectives Rosie and Ed, who were responsible for Carmen's arrest.

Anna found the detectives. She asked them what was holding up the paperwork to release Carmen. Ed and Rosie told Anna, "He has just been arrested. Please give us a chance to finish our paperwork. When we finish our paperwork we will give it to the desk sergeant so Carmen can be released." Anna went back to report to the Captain what she found out.

Needless to say, when she told the Captain what was holding up the paper work, Joseph didn't like what he heard. Joseph told the Captain, "I have never heard of anything so ridiculous in my life. What a stupid answer! What is taking the detectives so long to release Carmen's paperwork?" The Captain called the detectives and told them to please hurry up with the release papers for Carmen.

Meanwhile, Rudolpho arrived at Carmen's home. By the time he arrived there Philomena was a total mess. She was still very upset with what the women did to Carmen. She was also upset that they kept Carmen in jail. Rudolpho stayed with Philomena to try and calm her down. While he was at their home, he met Philomena's friend Rita. They started to talk together. They could not believe all the awful things that were happening to Carmen and Philomena.

Rita had been Philomena's friend for several years, and Rudolpho had been Carmen's friend for many years. Soon both of them started to collaborate on the things they could do to help these two people out. Rita told Rudolpho she was going to stay with Philomena until Carmen came home. Rudolpho said he was going to work the phones to see if he could find out how to get Carmen out of all this trouble.

Back at the police station, thanks to the Captain, Carmen's lawyer was finally able to get the paperwork on Carmen so he could be released. Carmen was never so glad to see Joseph as he was now. Carmen told Joseph that this is one place he didn't want to make his permanent residence.

Carmen told Joseph that the jail was full of bugs. He told Joseph he didn't know where to lean. He also told Joseph he could not sit on anything. He thought the bugs would get on him. Carmen thanked Joseph for coming to get him out of jail. He also thanked him for bringing him home.

As soon as Carmen got home Philomena grabbed him and gave him a huge hug and kiss. She was so glad to see him. Philomena told Carmen to come in the kitchen and she would make him something to eat.

Carmen also invited Joseph, Rita, and Rudolpho to come into the kitchen and told them Philomena would fix all of them something to eat. Philomena knew they all had something important to talk about. Philomena made them her famous Chicken Parmesan and spaghetti with her wonderful Marinara sauce.

This was a celebration for Carmen's return home from jail. It also started a relationship between Rita and Rudolpho. While Philomena was preparing the dinner, Carmen went to the wine cabinet and brought out his best Ruffino Classico Chianti. There was a wonderful celebration at the Del Judajea's home that evening.

CHAPTER TWENTY-FOUR
Carmen Sends Rudolpho to Investigate

Carmen told Rudolpho to go to Hampden and check out what was going on there. Carmen heard that someone had set up an operation over there to take book. Rudolpho went to Hampden to check out the situation.

As soon as Rudolpho got there, he ran into a man named Manny. Rudolpho believed the man lived in the area. Rudolpho approached the man and asked him if he had seen a tall man, who walked with a limp. Manny told Rudolpho that this man hangs out at the Rocket to Venus.

Rudolpho then asked Manny, "Do you think I can place a bet there?"

Manny told Rudolpho, "Yes, you definitely could place a bet there."

Rudolpho went to the restaurant to check out the situation. When he got there, he found out the place didn't open until five o'clock in the evening. He would have to come back later in the evening.

When Rudolpho came back to the restaurant, he sat at the bar and ordered a Natty Boh. He started a conversation with Frank the bartender. After a while, Rudolpho asked the bartender if he knew of a place in the area that took some action on football games. When the bartender heard this, he became curious.

Frank the bartender had never seen this man before and he didn't believe that he lived in the area. Frank could tell this by the way the man was asking him questions. This made Frank skeptical of giving him any answers about gambling on a football game.

Frank thought this man could be a cop. Therefore, Frank just changed the topic of conversation and started to talk about the place. Frank told Rudolpho the history of the restaurant. When Frank told Rudolpho about the Rocket to Venus, Rudolpho laughed. Rudolpho could not believe a person would try to go to Venus without knowing any details about it. Since Rudolpho could not find out any information from the bartender, he said his goodbyes and left.

Later in the evening, Donald came into the restaurant. Frank told Donald there was a strange man who had come into the restaurant and asked him about placing a bet on a football game. Frank told Donald that because he had never seen this man before, he never gave him any information. Donald told Frank that was very smart. When Donald heard this, he considered staying away from the restaurant for a while. Then he changed his mind. He thought why should he miss out on the action he was getting from this bar? Donald decided he would keep going to the bar to pick up the money from Frank for the bets he was taking from the customers.

After Donald got the money from Frank he took it over to the Little Italy bookies, Alberto and Joseph. Alberto and Joseph gave Donald his pay for the work he was doing for them. When Donald got his money, he told Alberto and Joseph that he had to have something for Frank the bartender also. Donald told Alberto and Joseph that Frank was getting all the bets for him.

Because this operation was running so smoothly, Alberto and Joseph wanted to expand it into different parts of Baltimore. Donald was running the operation for them. The bookies didn't want to take Donald off the operation. The bookies hated waves and they wanted every operation to run smoothly. Alberto and Joseph realized that they had to look for someone else to run their operation in a different location in Baltimore.

Since Donald had been in the Hampden area for some time, he had become very close to the bartenders there. Donald became friends with Colin and Alex because he was always at the restaurant. Donald felt closer to Frank because he was the first bartender who helped him. The two of them would go out together to different restaurants in the area when Frank was off. Frank tried to take his days off on Tuesdays and Wednesdays because there were no football games on those days.

On Tuesdays and Wednesdays Frank and Donald would go to dinner or to a movie together. They became good friends. Because they were always together, they formed a lasting friendship.

CHAPTER TWENTY-FIVE
The New Location for the Bookies

In the meantime the bookies from Little Italy, Alberto and Joseph, wanted to set up another one of their operations around the Pimlico Race Track. They knew there would be plenty of people going to the race track. They also knew these people liked to place bets. They wanted to cash in on some of the action in this area. They set their sights on one of their operations being located near the race track.

After a short drive to the area, they found out that the neighborhood around the Pimlico Race Track was considered a little shaky. They discussed it and decided to move a little farther away from the race track, but within the same vicinity. They decided to move up towards Randallstown to find a nice location to set up their operation.

Across the street from the Pimlico Hotel there was a man named Nookie the bookie. Nookie sat at the Wases Deli located at Park Heights and Haywood Avenue across from the Reisterstown Plaza. This was his headquarters. This is where he would collect the money that was owed to him or that he had to pay off. He carried out his business here because there was a phone booth next door to the deli. He believed that the phone booth was his personal phone booth. He wouldn't let anyone use it because he was waiting for people to call him to place their bets. Someone complained to the police that Nookie wouldn't let them use the phone booth. Because of the complaint the police locked him up.

There were many businesses on Liberty Road which made the area more appealing to the bookies. They figured many businesses meant many people. One of the places they were particularly interested in was a mattress store owned by friends from Little Italy. The bookies had known these people for some time. The Little Italy bookies met these people at their favorite restaurant in Little Italy. Seeing these people regularly, they became friends. Their names were Elliott and Eileen. The bookies had many things in common with these people. They all liked to gamble.

The bookies and the couple from the mattress store in Randallstown both loaned money to different people for a price. Every time they met in the restaurant they compared notes. They all talked about how they loaned money to people. They said when they did this they had a hard time getting their money back. They decided that from now on they would be careful who they loaned money to.

After discovering the similarities they both had Alberto and Joseph decided to visit Elliott and Eileen's store. They wanted to have a lengthy conversation with them. Elliott and Eileen are the buyers and sellers of their business. Many people came to buy things from them during the holidays and all year long. Elliott would also go to some of the people's home that lived in the area and sell them the merchandise that he had in his store. This proved to be very profitable for him. It provided a friendlier atmosphere between Elliott's clients and him.

Elliott and Eileen bought this store from Elliott's boss in 1977 because Elliott's boss wanted to retire. The business is on Liberty Road near the Key Bank, which was once called the Old Court Bank. It is also near the Northwest Hospital which was once called the Baltimore County Hospital. There is also the

Randallstown Elementary School which was where children in the area attended school.

In the past, the neighborhood was very nice. It consisted of all working class people. The people who lived in the area were predominately Jewish. A Chinese restaurnat is located up the street from the mattress store. The people from the mattress store often have dinner there.

Alberto and Joseph wanted to talk to Elliott and Eileen about something important. They wanted to know if there was a location in the area that would be good for them to set up their operation. As Alberto and Joseph arrived at Elliott and Eileen's store, they saw a fortune teller's business in front of the mattress business. After they went into the store, they asked Elliott and Eileen about the fortune teller. The bookies were wondering what kind of business the fortune teller had.

Elliott and Eileen told Alberto and Joseph how the fortune teller operated. The fortune teller could relay her conversations with customers to her son in another room via earphones. When the customer asked the fortune teller a question, all her son had to do was go on the computer and look up the answer. Then he would relay the answer to his mother. The mother had earphones on and she could hear everything that her son was telling her. The system worked well for them. This is why the fortune teller was always busy. When Alberto and Joseph heard this they all laughed.

Alberto and Joseph asked their friends the question that they really came there to ask them in the first place. Alberto and Joseph asked Elliott and Eileen if they knew of any place in the area that would be good for them to set up their numbers operation. Elliott and Eileen took them to a restaurant up the street from their store. The restaurant had been there for many years and had a fabulous following.

As they entered the restaurant, they were greeted by the hostess and were seated. The restaurant was a Chinese restaurant, and were known for the best Chinese food. They were seated in the main dining room and the waitress came over to greet them. She asked if they wanted anything to drink. Since it was lunch time they all ordered iced tea. After she came back with the tea they ordered food. They had Wonton soup, some of them had Sweet and Sour Chicken and the others had a seafood dish. The food was so delicious they really had a great lunch. When they were finished their meal, they had cheesecake for dessert. Alberto and Joseph enjoyed their dining experience as it was their first time being in this restaurant.

After they finished lunch Alberto and Joseph decided to go to the bar and have a drink. They asked Elliott and Eileen to join them. Alberto and Joseph really wanted to go to the bar so they could talk to the bartender. They were interested in setting up their operation there. This was the reason they wanted to go to the restaurant in the first place. They wanted to see what kind of a person the bartender was. If he was a nice person they could send their guy there to talk to the bartender. Alberto and Joseph struck up a conversion with the bartender, whose name was Reed. The bar had two TV's in it with all the different sport games on at all times.

As they were having their drinks they were able to talk to Reed for a while. Alberto and Joseph asked Reed what kind of a crowd came into the bar. Reed told Alberto and Joseph that it was mostly a young crowd that came to the bar. This made the bookies become even more interested after Reed told them this.

The bookies asked Reed if his customers were interested in the games that were on TV. Reed told the bookies that the customers are very interested in the games on TV. The only thing the customers were upset about was that they didn't know anyone to place a bet with. As soon as Alberto and Joseph heard this, they believed this place would work for them. The bookies told Elliott and Eileen they had the information they needed and that Reed had a great personality.

Alberto and Joseph came home and called their relative Tom and asked him to come to their home. They had a job they wanted him to do for them. The next day, Tom came to their home, and they proposed their offer to him. They told Tom they wanted him to go someplace and set up an operation for them. They told Tom it would be an easy job. Alberto and Joseph told Tom they wanted him to go to a Chinese restaurant in Randallstown to set up a numbers operation for them.

The bookies told Tom they went to the restaurant the other evening and talked to the bartender there whose name was Reed. While they talked to Reed at the restaurant they asked him if they knew of anyone who wanted to place bets on the games. Reed told us he knew plenty of people who wanted to do this.

Alberto and Joseph told Tom they wanted him to go to the restaurant and to make friends with Reed the bartender there. Alberto and Joseph told Tom that Reed was a very friendly person.

The bookies also told Tom, "The reason we wanted you to go there is because you are young, and you can relate to all the young people better than we can." The bookies asked Tom if he thought he could handle this without any problem. Tom told the bookies he would love to do this for them.

Tom was a go-getter and a very outspoken person. Tom didn't have any trouble relating to people of his own age. His relatives sent him there to be the spokesperson for them. Tom wanted to help his uncles Alberto and Joseph out. He believed it would be a new adventure for him. Tom stepped up to the plate and went to the restaurant and made friends with the bartender Reed. After

Tom made friends with Reed, the bartender set Tom up with some people who wanted to place bets. As soon as Reed did this for Tom, he began getting some action for his uncles Alberto and Joseph. Tom was young and energetic and he was just the right kind of person that Alberto and Joseph wanted to run their operation in Randallstown. Soon Tom had many regular customers that he took book from. After he acquired all of these customers, he reported back to his Uncles. Alberto and Joseph were very pleased with the work that Tom was doing. Soon Tom had a big winner in Randallstown, this helped him get more customers for his Uncles Alberto and Joseph.

The operation was running so smoothly that it made Alberto and Joseph want to extend their operation to another part of town. When Reed was not working at the restaurant Tom and Reed would go out and party together.

CHAPTER TWENTY-SIX
Carmen's Decision

Carmen found out the drug dealers were mixing the awful drug fentanyl with heroin. He worried that something serious could happen to his nephews. This situation haunted Carmen constantly. Carmen wanted to put a stop to these awful drugs. This was the main reason why Carmen resisted Alberto and Joseph's enthusiasm to sell the drugs. Carmen insisted he did not want to get involved with the damage that the drugs created.

Carmen tried to get his nephews into the treatment centers. Although he knew he was fighting a terrible situation, he wanted them to be well again. His nephews were resisting all the attempts that Carmen was doing to help them. Even though they were resisting Carmen's help, he was still trying to keep his nephews safe and healthy. Carmen worried for the children, and what would happen to them if they didn't have a father.

Carmen made up his mind he was going to talk to the detectives about what he found out about the drugs. He believed that after he told them this, then maybe they would believe he didn't want anything to do with drugs.

Carmen called Ed and Rosie and told them he had something he wanted to talk to them about. When Ed and Rosie arrived at the Del Judajea's home, Carmen told them immediately about what he found out about the drugs. He wanted to help them as much as possible. Carmen told the detectives he wanted to join forces with them, to put a stop to what was happening to the people that became strung out on drugs. He was very worried about his nephew's welfare after he found out what the drug dealers were doing. The detectives didn't realize how upset the Del Judajeas were for their nephews. They were under the impression the Del Judajeas were selling the drugs. They believed that was how their nephews got involved with drugs.

When the detectives heard this, they were in total shock. They were convinced that the Del Judajeas were the suppliers of all the drugs that were floating around the City. As a result, they were undecided whether or not to believe Carmen. They thanked Carmen for offering to help them, and they told him they would get back to him. With this new information, they left the Del Judajea's home and went to talk to the Captain.

When the detectives arrived at the Captain's office the Captain began telling them about all the drugs that were infesting the City. The Captain told the detectives that he surmised that the drug dealers had something to do with the women who were being hurt. The Captain informed the detectives that he added Ricky and Anthony to the investigation and that he wanted them to work together on this case. The detectives told the Captain they would do whatever it takes to stop the drugs from circulating in the City. Ed and Rosie were excited to work with Ricky and Anthony on this case.

Before they left the Captain's office, they told him what Carmen told them, about helping them put a stop to the drugs. The Captain told the detectives that this is a good thing, "If we have Carmen on our side maybe he could help us capture some of the drug dealers."

Most of the people who used these drugs were only interested in one thing. The reason they did this was to make themselves be able to function during the day. Of course, this wasn't the case.

They would become incoherent and go into convulsions at times. There were drug dealers and there were drug users. Most of the time they were the same people. They not only sold the drugs, they used them also. The environment in which to mix drugs were not sanitary. Dealers mixed the drugs in dirty basements or in their cars or sometimes on the steps in their neighborhood. Most dealers did not take any time measuring the amounts that they were mixing together. Some of the substances had more fentanyl in them and other capsules had less. Of course, the users were taking a huge risk on what they were putting into their bodies. The drug users were gambling with their lives. Usually the users were so strung out on drugs, they really didn't bother finding out what percentage of fentanyl was in the capsules they were buying. They were so addicted to the drug.

The heavy drug users lived in abandoned homes. These houses are called trap houses, and this is where some of the people went to mix the drugs. Some of the dealers were mixing the drugs with carfentanyl. This is worse than regular fentanyl. Carfentanyl is 10,000 times more potent than morphine and 100 times more potent than fentanyl. Most drug users didn't care who they got their drugs from. There was always an urgency to sell the drugs. They used the money they made on the sales to buy drugs for themselves.

The detectives knew they had to go after the drug dealers. The Captain told Ricky and Anthony to go to the infested area. The area the detectives were sent was very dangerous. It is located in West Baltimore. People were killing one another there. If the drug dealers caught someone else selling drugs on their corner, they started to fight with them, and one thing lead to another. Eventually someone would be hurt or even murdered.

Ricky and Anthony kept combing the area looking for the drug dealers who were mixing fentanyl with heroin. Ricky and

Anthony dressed undercover. They dressed with torn jeans and old dirty clothes. The detectives even put dirt on their face and arms when they mingled with the drug users. They acted like they were strung out on the drugs the same way the people acted who were hooked on drugs. They had been with these people for some time and they knew how they acted. It was easy for Ricky and Anthony to mingle with them, because they knew their actions.

When Ricky and Anthony went to West Baltimore, they couldn't find some of the people they had made friends with before. They had to delve further to see where the people they knew were. Ricky and Anthony were lucky they were able to hook up with someone they had met before. He was a little guy and he had a nice personality, considering the situation he was in. His name was John. John was always laughing. If you didn't know his situation, you would have thought he was a regular guy.

After they reconnected with John they asked him where he was getting his heroin from. John told them that he would go out of the area to get his drugs. He had a great connection in the east part of town. He didn't want to give up his suppliers. He was keeping this information to himself. After mingling with him for awhile, they finally learned where the drugs were coming from. When they questioned John further, he told them he got his drugs from Little Italy. As soon as Anthony and Ricky found this out, they reported back to Captain Dave. The detectives told the Captain that all the drugs were coming from the Little Italy bookies. Ricky and Anthony also told the other detectives it was the Little Italy bookies who were behind the drugs.

When Ricky and Anthony told Ed and Rosie this, they were surprised. They were still convinced that the Del Judajeas were the people behind the drugs. Ed and Rosie believed this because

Carmen's nephews were strung out on drugs. The detectives didn't realize how upset the Del Judajeas were because of what happened to their nephews.

Captain Dave sent floaters into Little Italy to see if they could find out more information. The floaters confirmed this to the Captain. It was also found that after the Little Italy people supplied the drugs, some dealers mixed the drugs with fentanyl. This was what was causing all the drug overdoses throughout the City.

Now Captain Dave had the necessary information about who was distributing the drugs throughout the City. He called Ed and Rosie into his office. He told them the people who were supplying these awful drugs were the Little Italy Bookies. Ed and Rosie told the Captain that Ricky and Anthony had confirmed this information. The detectives changed their attitude towards the Del Judajeas drastically.

CHAPTER TWENTY-SEVEN
Another Location for the Bookies

The location in Randallstown was really working out for the Little Italy bookies. They were so excited about what was happening in their new location. They wanted to have their operation working all over the City. Alberto and Joseph set their sights on a section of Roland Avenue.

Alberto met a man at the race track one day. Alberto found out the man, named Danny, was a meat cutter who worked at Eddie's Supermarket on Roland Avenue. After their first meeting they became friends, always talking about the horses at the Pimlico Race Track. They discussed which horse they thought was going to win. They would go back and forth on which horse they liked more that the other horses. These discussions would go on the whole time they were at the track. As a result of their many discussions, they become friends. While they were discussing the horses, Alberto asked Danny if he would be interested in taking some book for him at the super market. Danny thought about this for a while. Danny told Alberto that he was interested in doing this, but he wanted to get some money from him. Alberto told Danny that wouldn't be a problem. Alberto told Danny he would give him a kick back if he got some business for him. After Alberto told Danny this, they both agreed that this relationship would grow as time went on.

Eddie's Super Market is a gourmet super market. It is a family owned and operated business. They have been operating since 1944. They soon became known as Eddie's of Roland Park. They make their menus anyway the patrons request. They also supply gifts and flowers for their customers. They can't do enough for their customers. They kill their customers with kindness. Eddie's always pays attention to detail, detail and more detail. Because they supply such excellent service and food they are constantly busy. They cook the food they serve their customers right in the store. This way the customers can experience amazing aromas when they enter the store.

Renee Sherman and Folus Hillard were their most enthusiastic customers. They told everyone that they knew the people who owned Eddie's Super Market treated their customers wonderful. Renee always said that the owners would bend over backwards to please their customers.

When Danny started taking book for Alberto, things were working out smoothly. Danny couldn't believe the amount of people who wanted to place bets. Because Danny had worked at the store for some time, he knew most of the customers that came into the store by their name. All the people Danny approached about placing bets told him they had been looking for someone to do this for them for some time. Danny told the people he was the man to help them do this. His customers were excited when they found this out.

All Danny had to do was tell one person he could take bets from them. This information went through all the customers that came to the super market. Danny got so many people wanting to place bets that he had a hard time handling all of them. While Danny was doing this he also had to be cautious not to let these things interfere with his regular job.

Soon the bookies operation was getting bigger and better. The word was getting out around town about it. The detectives also heard about what was going on there. They sent their floaters to the store to find out about the operation. They wanted to know who was behind the operation. It didn't take the detectives long to find out who was behind the operation.

The detectives had always believed this operation belonged to the Del Judajeas. Rosie and Ed's investigation found out it wasn't the Del Judajeas after all. The detectives found out the meat cutter, Danny was behind this particular operation. The investigation further implicated the Little Italy bookies.

While the detectives found out that the Little Italy bookies had their operation going on in this part of town, they found out there was a huge operation going on in the Hampden area too. Further investigation revealed the operation was going on in a restaurant known as the Rocket to Venus.

The Captain sent Ed and Rosie to the restaurant to check the situation out. They told the Captain they would go to the Rocket to Venus to have something to eat. While the detectives were there, a tall man walked in. The man was very thin and they noticed he walked with a limp.

When the detectives saw this man it immediately made them think of the women who had been injured by a man who walked with a limp. The detectives kept watching to see what this person was doing. The man went directly to the bar and started to have a lengthy conversation with the bartender. When the detective's waitress, Elizabeth, came to their table, they asked her who was the man at the bar talking to the bartender. Elizabeth told the detectives, "Oh that man. He is a friend of the bartenders."

Ed and Rosie called Captain Dave and told him they thought they have finally found the man matching the description of the suspect who was beating the women up. They told the Captain to send some police to the restaurant and take this man in for questioning. With Ed and Rosie's advice, Captain Dave sent his police to the restaurant to bring the man in for questioning.

Ed and Rosie stayed in the restaurant and just observed what the man was doing with the bartender. The detectives kept a watchful eye on the two men. Finally the police entered the restaurant. They walked up to the bar and told the man they wanted to bring him in for some questioning.

The police took the man down to the police station and the detectives paid their check. The two went to the bar to have a drink.

They asked the bartender, "Boy what just happened? Was that man a friend of yours?"

The bartender told them, "Yes, he was a friend of mine." He also told the detectives he didn't know why the police came after him. The bartender told the detectives the man was a frequent customer at the restaurant.

The detectives asked the bartender what kind of business the man was in. The bartender told the detectives that he didn't know.

Ed said to the bartender, "He was your friend and he came here all the time and you're telling me you don't know what kind of business this man was in?"

The bartender told Ed, "No I don't know what he does for a living."

The bartender continued to say that all he knew, was that the man came to the restaurant all the time. Frank the bartender told the detectives that was why they became friends. Frank told the detectives he was a good tipper and that's why he liked the man. The detectives thought this was a little odd. If the man was a regular customer why didn't the bartender know what kind of business the man was in?

Ed and Rosie left the bar and they called Captain Dave back. They told the Captain they thought they should come back to the restaurant and bring the bartender in for questioning also. Ed and Rosie told the Captain the bartender was good friends with the man with the limp. They also told the Captain that when they asked the bartender what the man did for a living, he told them he didn't know.

With the information received from the two detectives, the Captain sent the police back to the restaurant to bring the bartender Frank in for questioning. Captain Dave hoped that with these two people brought in for questioning he might be able to find something out.

The detectives had the police put the suspect in one room and the bartender in another. Rosie and Ed went into the room the man with the limp was in. They found out the man's name was Donald. First they read him his rights. They didn't want to mess anything up. They asked him if he wanted anything to drink and he told them he would like to have a glass of water. This was perfect because the detectives thought after he drank the water they could get his DNA.

When they gave Donald his drink Rosie and Ed tried to make a connection with him. They told him he had the right to a lawyer and he immediately replied that he had a lawyer. They wanted to be able to question him without any restraints. They began by asking him simple questions; his name, address, and what did he do for a living. When the detectives asked Donald his name he had no problem answering them. The detectives asked him his address he didn't have a problem answering them. But when they asked him what he did for a living he hesitated and started to stutter. The detectives had a feeling that what they suspected about this man was true. They believed he was working for the bookies.

Now that the man that walked with a limp was in the station, the Captain got in touch with the three women who had been assaulted. He told the women he wanted them to come into the police station. He told the women he found a tall man who walked with a limp and he wanted them to take a look at the man. The women were happy when the Captain told them this.

The women told the Captain they would be glad to come in and look at the man providing the man could not see them. Captain Dave assured the women the man would not be able to see them. With this assurance from the Captain, the women came in to look at the suspect. The Captain had the man in a room where the women could look in and see him but he could not see them. As soon as the women saw the man they all screamed and put their hands over their mouths. This confirmed that he was the culprit to the Captain.

They asked Captain Dave, "Are you sure he can't come after us anymore?"

Captain Dave told the women, "Now that you all have identified the man we can hold him here. He won't be able to hurt any of you again."

The women were very relieved that the man was finally caught. The women thought they would finally be able to go home tonight and sleep peacefully with their children.

Anna, the Captain's secretary, told Rosie and Ed to come into Captain Dave's office, he wanted to talk to them. When Ed and Rosie came into the Captain's office they were informed, "We have positive identification from the victims that this was the man who hurt them." The two detectives hurried back to further question Donald.

When Ed and Rosie got back into the room that Donald was in they asked him, "Why were you hurting these women? What was the reason you did this to them? You must have had a motive to do this to them. What was it?"

Donald wouldn't budge. He knew that as long as he didn't say anything they couldn't hold him. What Donald didn't know was that they had the eyewitness description from the women who he attacked.

Rosie told Donald, "The three women have already been down to the police station and identified you as the man who hurt them. Now what have you got to say for yourself?"

Donald insisted that he wanted to talk to his lawyer.

"Ok," the detectives told Donald, "You want to talk to a lawyer? If you do this, the deal is off the table." Ed and Rosie asked Donald again, "Are you sure you want to talk to a lawyer?" Donald thought about this for a couple of minutes, but insisted that he still wanted to talk to his lawyer.

The detectives left Donald in the room by himself and went to talk to their Captain. The Captain told them to let Donald talk to his lawyer. Consequently, they went back to Donald and let him call his lawyer, Mr. Kleeman.

CHAPTER TWENTY-EIGHT
The Little Italy Neighborhood

A man named Omar was born in New York City in 1980. His family came from Jordan. He lived between New York and New Jersey with his parents for some time. Omar went to school in New Jersey at Baruck College. He had a fabulous teacher whose name was Phyllis Bagley. She liked Omar a lot and watched out for him, because she knew he was a good person. When he graduated from college, Phyllis got him a job working with computers.

She called him and told him she had a great job for him in Baltimore. The company was located in Little Italy in Baltimore, Maryland. He got the job so he began to look for a place to live near where he worked. Omar didn't know anything about Baltimore. He took buses everywhere.

He got an apartment in West Baltimore, an area he knew nothing about. After he was there for a while, he noticed what was happening in the area. He started to look for another apartment. One day, when he left work, he walked into Little Italy to get some change. He had to catch a bus. He had an appointment to look at an apartment in Canton. He stopped at a store that was owned by a man named Mugs. When Mugs asked Omar if he wanted anything, Omar told Mugs the only thing he needed was some change.

Mugs became upset because Omar only wanted change. Omar told Mugs he had to catch a bus because he was looking

for an apartment. Mugs told him there was an apartment in a home in Little Italy that was for rent. Mugs told Omar that he should go and check it out. Omar went to see the apartment. Later he told Mugs he liked it. Mugs told Omar, "You like it, then you can rent it." Mugs continued, "The home belongs to me."

The rental agreement created a lasting friendship between Omar and Mugs. Mugs watched out for Omar because he knew Omar was not familiar with the American ways.

Mugs had been in business for many years. Mugs sold subs, lunch meat, cheese, bread, milk, and sodas in his store. He knew everyone who lived in Little Italy and beyond. Mugs knew everything that was happening in the neighborhood. Mugs' store became the place to go. People of all ages would hang out around Mugs' corner store. They knew if they hung around the store, they would be able to find out what was going on in the neighborhood. The young people in the neighborhood wanted to be where the action was. They also knew if a job offer came up they would be there to apply for the job.

Once, Mugs got Tony Perrera to do some major construction work for him on his store. The bookies were going to have card games upstairs in Mugs' store. Tony did everything that Mugs asked him to do to complete the project. Finally the project was completed.

Mugs also knew all the bookmakers in Little Italy. He was friends with all of them. Mugs was known as being a very wise man. He was older and had been around a while. He had a lot of experience in many different situations. He knew about Alberto and Joseph's operation. Mugs told them he thought it was a bad idea. He told them it was too dangerous.

Mugs knew if Alberto and Joseph got involved with drugs that it would be a more serious offense than just taking bets. Mugs told Alberto and Joseph that they should just stick to numbers. Of course, Alberto and Joseph didn't listen to him. They had a backer who was constantly urging them to sell drugs. They needed to please their main man. Mugs did not know this.

When Mugs' bookie friends couldn't handle all the bets, they would pass them on to Mugs. Occasionally he would do some favors for the bookies in the neighborhood. Several times Mugs took some book on the side also. The police knew he did this too. They raided Mugs' place all the time, but they never could find any evidence he was taking book. The police were very frustrated because they could not catch Mugs.

One time, the cops planned a big raid on Mugs' store. They brought a big truck with them to the store. There was a phone booth inside Mugs' store. Written all over the phone booth were Mug's bookie friend's names and numbers. The cops got their workers to take the whole phone booth out of Mugs' store. The cops destroyed everything that Tony had built or restored for Mugs in a matter of minutes.

There was another place in Little Italy where all the local bookies hung out during the day. There was a mailbox located on the corner outside a sub shop. The bookies leaned on the mail box during the day. People would come up to them and place bets with them. When the bookies saw the cops coming near them they put all the pieces of paper with the numbers on them inside the mailbox. When the mailman came to collect the mail from inside the mailbox, the mailman found all these little pieces of paper crumbled up inside the mailbox. He didn't know what they were so he threw them all away. What these papers had on them were all the numbers that the people placed bets on earlier during the day. The people who placed the bets that day probably did not win. If they won, they never got paid.

Ralphino was a local bookie that lived in the neighborhood. He had a wonderful personality and everybody liked him. Ralphino was a very plain man. He was very thin and dressed very modestly. To look at Ralphino, you would never know he was one of the biggest bookies that lived in Little Italy. When you hit on the number you bet with him, Ralphino paid you right away. All the people liked him because they never had to argue with him if they won.

Ralphino also cautioned Alberto and Joseph not to sell drugs because it was too dangerous. He told Alberto and Joseph that they were going down a very dangerous road.

One time a young girl came to the restaurant in Little Italy who read cards. She had a fantastic personality, and when Kathy spoke with her she found out that she was a card reader. Kathy asked her if she could read her cards. She told her she could. Since it was extremely busy in the restaurant that evening, Kathy asked her if it would be possible for her to come back on another day. She explained to her that Sunday evening around ten o'clock would be a better time for her to come because it was slower then. Kathy would be able to talk to her with more ease then.

When Sunday came, the owner of the restaurant's brother asked him if he could borrow twenty dollars because he wanted to get in the poker game. The game was across the street from the restaurant. The owner lent his brother the money for him to get in the game. Later that evening the little card reader returned to Sabatino's restaurant. Kathy was very happy to see her. When her bosses found out she was a card reader they told her that she had to read their cards first. The little girl read Kathy's two bosses' cards. At the end of every reading she told them that a man in uniform was coming to visit the restaurant. They all thought about this and came up with the same idea. They told the little girl that none of them knew anyone who was in the service.

Around midnight that evening, one of Kathy's bosses went out front of the restaurant to get some fresh air. What he saw was unbelievable. The cops were climbing the walls of the building across the street with sawed off shot guns. Kathy's boss didn't know what was happening. All of a sudden several older men came running out of the building. There was a paddy wagon outside the building and the police were rounding up all the older men to put them inside it.

When the men saw Kathy's boss from the restaurant, they tried to hand him their money. They didn't want to take the money downtown with them. Kathy's boss gave the men shots of VO before the cops put them into the paddy wagon. It was a site to behold.

No one could understand why the police were so interested in some older men playing poker for money. There were more serious criminal activities going on in town that the cops could have investigated. They chose to raid a building that had a group of older men playing poker. The police thought this was more important than checking out the serious crimes happening in town.

Later that evening when all the men were taken away, Kathy finally realized what the little card reader was trying to tell her and her bosses. When she told us a man in uniform was coming to see them, it wasn't a man from the armed services. All along she was trying to tell them it was the police. It was unbelievable!

CHAPTER TWENTY-NINE
The Deli Manager

Alberto and Joseph's big benefactor was calling back some of the favors that he had been giving them. He continued to be on their backs about selling drugs. Their benefactor kept asking them, "What is holding you up? When are you going to start to do this?" The benefactor told Alberto and Joseph, "Let's get started with my project." Little Italy's benefactor wanted to make more and more money. As a result of the pressure, the Little Italy bookies had to go to their workers.

The Little Italy bookies told their workers they wanted them to start to sell drugs. When they told their workers this they were very surprised that none of their workers wanted to get involved with drugs. The workers knew that the bookie's operation was just a misdemeanor. If they got involved in drugs it would be a bigger offense. None of the workers for the Little Italy bookies wanted to be involved in selling drugs. There was only one person who was willing to do this for them and that was Donald.

When the Little Italy bookies found out that Donald was willing to deal, they told him to tell his workers to start selling drugs. As expected, some of Donald's workers were undecided about doing this. They knew it would be more dangerous than just taking book. Alberto and Joseph wanted to please their benefactor.

The bookies went to their contact, Danny, from the grocery

store. They asked him if he knew of any people who would be interested in buying drugs. Danny told them he would have to check around. Danny told Alberto he didn't know anyone who did drugs and he didn't do drugs himself. None of the people that he knew wanted any drugs. Danny could not help to get any customers for Alberto and Joseph.

Alberto and Joseph contacted their benefactor and told him what was happening. Their benefactor was upset when he heard this. He didn't care about whose lives would be hurt, he just wanted to make a profit.

Meanwhile, at the police station, the Captain found out that Eddie's Super Market had some gambling activity going on there. He sent Ed and Rosie there to investigate the situation. When they arrived, they were amazed at all the wonderful smells they experienced when they entered the store. This made the detectives hungry so they went to the deli to buy some food. They talked to Danny the deli man and asked him what was good to eat. Danny told the detectives that just about everything was good for them to eat. Danny asked them what did they like and then he would tell them what to get. Finally the detectives were able to get some great food.

While the detectives were there, they noticed there was a lot of activity going on with Danny and some of the customers. They started to pay more attention to the activity that was going on there. They realized that the customers were placing bets with Danny. The detectives began to wonder if there was a connection between Danny and the bookies.

After they finished their meal, they called the Captain and told him to send some police to arrest the deli manager. The detectives told the Captain they saw the deli manager take bets from some of his customers. The Captain sent some police to the store to bring Danny the deli manager in for questioning.

They put Danny in one of the interrogating rooms. When Ed and Rosie came in to question him, Danny said to them, "Weren't you the two people who were just in the store?" The detectives told him he was correct. They thanked him for the food and told him it was great. Then the two detectives started to question him. They asked him what his job was at the store. Danny told the detectives he was the deli manager.

Next Ed asked Danny, "We observed you taking bets from some of the customers. Was that your job also?"

Danny began to stutter. He didn't want to incriminate himself. He knew he was in trouble if he answered them. He told the detectives he wanted to talk to his lawyer.

Ed told Danny, "You know if you talk to a lawyer we will not be able to help you anymore."

Danny still insisted that he wanted to talk to his lawyer. Danny called Elaine Sweiber Katz. Elaine came to the police station and she asked to talk to her client Danny. They took Elaine to the room that Danny was in. Elaine didn't know that the detectives had a microphone in the room. She asked her client what information the police had on him. Danny told Elaine that they have him taking bets on some of his customers at the store.

Elaine told Danny, "Well I'll see if I can get you off of that." She told Danny that this is just a misdemeanor and it shouldn't be any problem for her to get him out of there. At the end of their conversation Elaine started the process to get Danny out of jail.

CHAPTER THIRTY
Frank the Bartender Goes
in for Questioning

Now that the detectives had enough evidence to hold Donald, they brought the bartender Frank in for questioning also. The detectives had the police put Donald in one room and the bartender Frank in another. The detectives were carrying a lot of papers in their hands when they entered the room to interrogate Frank the bartender. They noticed he was extremely nervous.

Frank had never been arrested before. He didn't have any idea about what was going to happen to him. The detectives read him his rights and also asked if he needed to talk to a lawyer, they would provide one for him. Frank told the detectives he had a lawyer. The detectives also asked Frank if he wanted anything to drink. Frank told them he would like to have a glass of water. After they read Frank his rights, the detectives started questioning him.

The detectives proceeded to question Frank and they could tell that he was ready to explode. They asked Frank what he was doing with Donald. How did the two of them become such good friends?

The detectives told the bartender, "Come on Frank. There has to be some big connection between the two of you."

The bartender became more and more nervous as the detectives continued to question him. Frank was a mess. He was not used to being interviewed about his personal life from someone in authority.

Frank finally asked "Can I talk to my lawyer?"

The detectives were surprised when he asked them this. They told him, "Yes you can talk to your lawyer, but after you do this we will not be able to help you anymore."

Even though Frank asked them if he could talk to his lawyer the detectives kept questioning him. They badgered him, "Come on Frank, tell us what the relationship was between the two of you." They knew they were stretching their luck by continuing to question Frank.

Eventually Frank confessed, "Donald approached me at the restaurant and asked me if I would like to make some extra money. I told Donald, 'Yes, I would love to make some extra money. What do I have to do?'" Donald told me, "All you have to do is ask some customers that came into the restaurant if they want to place bets on the games and numbers." Frank told the detectives, "That's all it was."

The detectives said, "Are you sure that's all it was?"

Frank answered the detectives, "Yes, at first that's all he wanted me to do for him."

The detectives asked Frank, "What else were you doing with him?"

Frank continued, "Donald asked me if I knew of any people who wanted to buy some drugs. I told him that I didn't know anyone who wanted to buy drugs."

The detectives left Frank and went to talk to the Captain. They told the Captain everything that the bartender told them. Captain Dave was very pleased with the detective's information learned from the bartender. The Captain asked the detectives if they had this information on tape. Ed and Rosie told the Captain yes, they had the tape going the whole time while they were interrogating the bartender.

The detectives told the Captain the bartender requested to talk to his lawyer. The Captain said that's okay. Let him talk to his lawyer now that we have all the information that we need on Donald and him.

Ed and Rosie went back to the bartender and told him he could call his lawyer. Frank called his lawyer, Stanley Alpert.

Mr. Alpert came to the police station looking for his client. He asked the police if he could talk to his client, Frank, the bartender from the restaurant "The Rocket to Venus." The detectives took Mr. Alpert in to see his client. Mr. Alpert entered the room that Frank was in and asked him what they were holding him for. Frank told Mr. Alpert everything that he told the detectives. When the lawyer heard this, he became upset.

The lawyer asked the bartender, "Why did you tell them all of that? Why didn't you talk to me first before you answered any of their questions?"

The bartender told Mr. Alpert he was so nervous he didn't know what to do. The lawyer told the bartender, "Now they have all the evidence you provided them with."

Mr. Alpert told Frank that he really gave him a rough job to get him out of the mess that he put himself in. The lawyer told the bartender, he wanted to see the transcript of his conversation with the detectives.

Mr. Alpert told the bartender, "After I see what you told them, then I will be able to figure out what I have to do to help you."

Mr. Alpert went to see what the detectives had on Frank. The lawyer wanted to see if they recorded the whole conversation between the detectives and the bartender. Little did Mr. Alpert know that the detectives had everything on tape, even Mr. Alpert's conversation with Frank.

CHAPTER THIRTY-ONE
Donald's Interrogation

Donald's life had seen many turns of events, starting from when he was young. He fell out of a tree, leaving him with a bad leg. Because of his bad leg, he couldn't play ball with his friends. That's when he got involved with the Little Italy bookies. When he got older and he had been around the bookies for some time, he started placing bets with Carmen because he paid better.

He believed Carmen owed him money, so he started to stalk Carmen's relatives. Rudolpho had his men take care of Donald. After Rudolpho's men handled Donald, he knew he had to leave this part of town. That's when Donald started working with the Little Italy bookies.

Due to this association, he got involved in many different things. The Little Italy bookies wanted him to take book and also sell drugs. With little concern for his life now, he did whatever the Little Italy bookies wanted him to do. Donald set up operations all over town for the Little Italy bookies and he was making a lot of money for them.

The Little Italy bookies insisted that Donald start to sell drugs for them. Donald looked at this as a new adventure for him. He soon made friends with the bartenders in Hampden.

The other person pressuring the Little Italy bookies to sell drugs was their benefactor. Even though the Little Italy bookies knew what their benefactor asked them to do was wrong, they did what he wanted them to do. He had been fronting them money for some time and without him they wouldn't have been so well-off.

Donald knew he was in trouble. Ed and Rosie returned to continue the questioning.

Ed asked Donald, "What were you doing in the restaurant? Who are you working for? Who put you up to taking book and selling drugs in the restaurant? Did you do this on your own or did someone put you up to this?"

Donald wouldn't help them. He knew as long as he didn't say anything they couldn't hold him. He just let the detectives do all the talking. He was taking everything in that they were saying to him.

Next the detectives asked, "Are you going to answer us or are you just going to sit there and say nothing?" The detectives said, "Come on Donald. There has to be some connection between the bartender and you. What was it?" The detectives continued, "Are you going to answer us? What is wrong with you Donald?"

Donald had already told them he wanted to talk to his lawyer. Donald waited for his lawyer to show up. Steve Kleeman came to the police station and asked to talk to his client. The police took the lawyer back to the interview room Donald was in.

Mr. Kleeman came into the room and immediately asked Donald what they had on him. Donald told the lawyer that he didn't say a word to them. Donald said he just let them do all the talking. The lawyer told Donald that was very wise. Little did either of them know, that the bartender told the detectives everything that Donald and he were doing.

The lawyer asked to speak to the detectives. Mr. Kleeman asked the detectives what they had on his client. Ed and Rosie told the lawyer everything that the bartender told them. When the lawyer heard what the bartender told them, he was in shock. Mr. Kleeman knew that Donald was in a lot of trouble. Mr. Kleeman had to do some powerful explaining to get Donald off of these charges. Mr. Kleeman wanted to get Donald released from the police station, but the detectives wanted to keep him there for further questioning. The detectives told the lawyer that Donald wouldn't answer any of their questions.

The detectives told Mr. Kleeman there was something else he should be aware of. Kleeman asked the detectives, "What else do you have on my client?" The detectives told Mr. Kleeman that the women who were beaten a while ago came into the police station and identified Donald as the person who hurt them. Mr. Kleeman was really upset when he heard this. He knew he had to do a lot of work to defend his client.

Mr. Kleeman went back into the room that Donald was in and told him what the detectives had on him. Donald became very upset. He knew he was in serious trouble now. He didn't know how his lawyer was going to get him out of all this trouble. Donald's lawyer told him he was going to go back to his office to do some research in the law books and see what he could find out to help him. Donald realized that his life had been one bad mistake after another. He blamed this reason why his life was in such an awful situation.

CHAPTER THIRTY-TWO
The Meeting

Every year, during the month of August, the residents of Little Italy have a huge festival for Saint Gabriel. Saint Gabriel is the patron Saint of their church in Little Italy. There are booths in the streets where people sell their special items. The residents of Little Italy make fried dough, a huge piece of dough covered with powdered sugar or granulated sugar. They also make home-made meatballs and spaghetti, sausage, peppers and onions, and of course, pizza. The money they raise during the festival goes to help Saint Leo's Church.

Many people from all over the City come to Little Italy for the festival. They come to eat the wonderful food, dance, and purchase some of the items that vendors are selling there. It is a fabulous time for all the people who attend the festival. There are bands playing music on a band stand that festival goers sing along to. People also dance in the street to the music that is played.

The Little Italy bookies were getting so greedy. All they were interested in was making more and more money. Of course they had their big benefactor that was constantly after them to sell drugs. He always told them there was more money in drugs than in numbers.

Their main man had a big tire business that is nationally owned. It was located in downtown Baltimore. Because of this location it was easy for him to come to Little Italy to talk to the bookies. The Little Italy benefactor even knew many politicians. He often donated a lot of money to their causes. Because he did this, he believed he had plenty people who would help him if he ever got into trouble. Their main man was the person who had been pulling all the strings and was telling the Little Italy bookies what to do and when to do it.

The Little Italy bookie's benefactor decided it was time to have a meeting with them in Little Italy. The day their benefactor decided to meet Alberto and Joseph was the same day of the Saint Gabriel's Festival. They scheduled the meeting to be held at their favorite restaurant in Little Italy. On this day though, the whole area was busy with people coming and going to the festival.

The Little Italy bookies had reserved a table in a section in the restaurant that was secluded from the rest of the customers. The owners of the restaurant took very good care of the Little Italy bookies because they were regular customers. The Little Italy bookies wanted to have a private meeting with their benefactor. Their benefactor didn't want anyone to know he was involved with the bookies from Little Italy. It was important to be a very private meeting.

Coincidently, on this same day Captain Dave, Ed and Rosie and some of the other police met at the same restaurant. The Captain wanted to talk to his officers about the people they recently arrested. While the Captain and the detectives were talking, Julian Jimmott and Ed Williams, who patrol the area, came in and joined them. The chance meeting of all these people to be in the same restaurant on this day was a total accident.

The Little Italy bookie benefactor arrived at the restaurant with his bodyguards. The benefactor and his two bodyguards all carried 45's under their coats. The benefactor's bodyguards looked like boxers. They were tall and huge and their muscles were bulging out of their coats. The reason the benefactor had the bodyguards with him today was because he was carrying something special. The benefactor wanted to call back some of the favors that he had given the Little Italy bookies over these many years. This was the whole reason why the benefactor wanted them to sell drugs. He wanted to get some of his money back.

The benefactor was a very boisterous person. He spoke a little louder than anyone else did in the room. The benefactor was insisting that the Little Italy bookies keep pressuring their workers to sell drugs. Alberto and Joseph replied to their main man that some of their workers didn't want to do this.

Alberto and Joseph told their benefactor that only one of their workers was willing to sell drugs for them. The workers knew that taking book is a misdemeanor, but selling drugs is a felony.

He said, "What do you mean you were only able to get one of your workers to do this? Don't they all work for you?"

The bookies said, "Well yes, they do work for us, but they don't want to get involved with drugs."

Then the benefactor asked them, "Who is the boss? You or them? You are supposed to be the boss, but they must be the boss." Of course, as he was saying this he became more and more upset and more loud and boisterous.

The benefactor said, "How can you guys sit there so calmly and tell me you can't get your workers to do this for you? I have been fronting you all of this money for years. After all I have done to help you guys out! This is unbelievable. I have even brought you a quarter pound of coke for you to give to your workers today. Now what am I supposed to do with it? This is the reason why I have my two friends with me today." The benefactor became more boisterous than ever. He spoke louder than anyone else did in the restaurant.

Captain Dave and his officers Ed and Rosie heard everything the loud conversation had to offer! The Captain called the station. The Captain told the desk sergeant to send a wagon down to Little Italy immediately. He told the desk sergeant he was going to need someone to stand by because he might have some criminals for them to take in.

The Captain was waiting for the big guy to leave. When the Captain and the other officers saw the benefactor and his men get up, they also got up. They were ready to arrest the big guy. As soon as the big guy came down the steps, he saw the cops and the other men. The benefactor didn't know that one of the people was the Captain of the police because he was in street clothes.

The big guy said, "What do you people want? Get out of my way. I am leaving this place."

The Captain said, "I don't think you are going anywhere without us."

The big guy replied, "Oh yes I am. I have my two guards with me."

Captain Dave wouldn't let them pass. This caused a commotion in the restaurant. The owners came over to help the police. When the owners found out what was happening they sent an employee outside to find some more police. They knew there had to be some police outside of their restaurant and they were right. Soon the restaurant was surrounded with the police, they were everywhere.

When they saw the Captain in the middle, they all jumped into action. Soon they had the big guy and his two thugs in custody. The confrontation was over in no time at all. The paddy wagon arrived outside and took the bad guys away.

Soon the restaurant was back to normal operation. The Captain went to talk to the Little Italy bookies. He said to them, "What are you guys doing? Aren't you in enough trouble that you have to start doing other things?"

The Little Italy bookies didn't know what to say. They were so upset after being confronted by the Captain they didn't know what to do. The Captain told them they had twenty four hours to straighten their act up. If they didn't do what he told them to do he was coming back to take them in. The Little Italy bookies were beside themselves. They knew they had to do something or else their benefactor would do something to them. Alberto and Joseph realized that the bookies from East Baltimore were right. They should have stuck to a good thing instead of going after something that was way far out of their reach.

THE END

Mrs. Philomena Del Judajea's

RECIPES

Please enjoy the following recipes
that are mentioned in the book

Chicken Noodle Soup

3   Chicken thighs, deboned and skinless
    (Chicken thighs have the sweetest meat)

4   Cups chicken broth

1   Large onion

8   Stalks of celery

30 Baby carrots

1/3 Tsp pepper

3   Tsp salt

4   Tbsp of parsley

1   Package of egg noodles

Fill a 12 quart pot with water to the level of the handles. Bring to a simmer. Add chicken and cook for 1 hour

Peel and dice the onion and add to pot.

Cut celery in half then cut in thirds. (It's preferable to leave the leaves on as they add flavor). Peel and cut the baby carrots then cut in half and add to the pot.
Add pepper, salt and parsley.

Cook for 1 hour more.

Remove and shred chicken. Return to pot.

Cook egg noodles in separate pot according to directions. Strain and add to chicken pot.

(Optional) Mrs. Del Judajea always added 1 8oz. can of tomato puree

Marinara Sauce

4 Tbsp Extra virgin olive oil

1 Large onion peeled and diced

4 Tbsp crushed garlic

3 Large cans crushed tomatoes (28 oz)

2 Tbsp parsley

16 Pieces of fresh basil leaves

1 Cup of chicken broth

1/3 Tsp of pepper

2 Tsp of salt

2 Tsp of sugar

(Optional) 1/2 Tbsp red pepper flakes

Sauté the onion in olive oil. Add the garlic and all the other seasonings. Add the 3 cans of crushed tomatoes.

Bring to a slight boil then turn it down and simmer on low for 1 hr. continually stirring it.

Homemade Pasta

3   Extra large eggs

3-4 Cups of all purpose flour

2-4 Tbsp of water

1   Tbsp olive oil

1   Tsp Salt

Beat the eggs well in a large bowl. Add 1 cup of flour and a dash of salt. Beat the ingredients till well blended. Work in remaining flour and water. Knead the dough gently and divide the dough in half. Then divide the dough into little sections. Push the dough through the pasta machine's widest setting, all the while sprinkling flour on the dough. Repeat rolling the dough through the machine until the desired thickness is reached. Lay the thin pieces on the table and sprinkle them with flour. Place the noodles in a 3 qt. pot of boiling water. Add 1 Tsp of salt & 1 tbsp olive oil. Cook the noodles for 2 to 3 min. until tender.

Serves 6

Meatballs

5   lbs of ground round

3   Eggs, beaten well

5   Tbsp of milk (optional)

1½ Tbsp oregano

2   Tbsp parsley

1½ Tbsp salt

10 pcs. fresh basil diced

5   Tsp crushed garlic

¼   Tsp pepper

8   Slices white bread, diced

Preheat the oven to 350 degrees

Beat eggs well. Add milk. Add the meat, all the seasonings and diced bread. Mix together until everything is blended. Roll the meatballs while you are waiting for the oven to heat. Bake in oven for twenty to thirty minutes. When they are finished place the meatballs in bowl and pour sauce on them.

Pasta e Fagoli

2   Large onions peeled, sliced and diced

6   Stalks of celery including the leaves

2   Large cans of chicken broth

2   2 lb bags of lima beans

2   Boxes of frozen spinach

½   Box elbow macaroni

1½ Tbsp of salt

1½ Tbsp of oregano

10 Pcs diced basil

2   Tbsp of parsley

½   Tsp dry hots

In a 12 qt. pot place all the ingredients except spinach and elbow macaroni. Fill the pot to the handles with cold water. Cook for 2 hours, then add spinach. Cook for another hour. Cook the macaroni in a different pot of boiling water until tender. Add the macaroni to all the other ingredients.

Serves 6

Chicken Parmesan

Large Chicken breast (pound the chicken breast)

Flour

Egg

Bread Crumbs

Parmesan cheese

Olive oil

Dip chicken breast into flour, then beaten egg. Then dip it in bread crumbs. Sauté the Chicken in olive oil until brown on both sides. Place cheese on the Chicken and place in the oven until the cheese melts. Add Marinara sauce.

Pizzelle Cookies

6 Large eggs
1¾ Cups of sugar
1 Cup butter
½ Bottle vanilla extract
½ Bottle anisette extract or anisette
3½ Cups all purpose flour
1 Tsp baking powder
Powdered sugar

Spray oil on the iron as needed. Beat eggs at medium speed. Add sugar and beat until thick. Add butter, vanilla, and anisette. Mix well. Add flour and baking powder. Beat until smooth.

Spray pizzelle iron and heat for 2 minutes. Place 1 teaspoon of dough on each cookie plate. Press iron closed.

Cook for 30 to 40 seconds or until desired color. When you take the cookies out you have to sprinkle powdered sugar on them right away so it sticks to the cookie.

Makes about 3½ dozen cookies

Mrs. Del Judajea's Italian Cookies

DOUGH:

7 Cups flour
7 Eggs
1 lb butter
1 Tbsp baking powder
2 Tsp vanilla
2 Tsp anise oil
½ Tsp salt
1 Box 10x sugar

ICING:

1 Cup 10x sugar
2 Tbsp milk
1/4 Tsp vanilla extract

Mix the dough and refrigerate 4 hrs. or overnight before making cookies. Remove dough and make 48 small balls. Roll each ball into a thin line and twist into pretzel shape. Bake at 350 degrees for 10-15 minutes.

Makes 4 dozen cookies

ICING:

Mix ingredients together. Dip or spread on cookies and sprinkle with sugar crystals.

Eggplant Parmesan

Eggplant

Marinara sauce

Egg

Flour

Shredded Parmesan cheese

Olive oil

Peel the eggplant and cut it into long pieces.

Dip the eggplant in egg and then dip it in flour. Fry the eggplant in the oil, but not too well done.

Layer the eggplant in a pan and put the Marinara sauce on top of it.

Put shredded cheese on top. Keep repeating layers until the eggplant fills the pan.

Bake in the oven at 350 degrees for 30 minutes. Check the eggplant after 20 minutes.

The recipe was given to me by Ricky Velleggia from his parents & grandparents

Strawberries Alberto

Strawberries

Red wine (Merlot or Lambrusco)

Lemon

1 Tsp Sugar

Clean & cut the strawberries into a bowl.

Add red wine to cover the strawberries. Add a teaspoon of sugar. Add a couple of lemon slices and squeeze them on the strawberries.

Stir and refrigerate.

Albert Isella's recipe

ABOUT
THE
AUTHOR
Leonora "Peachy" Dixon

Baltimore's very own Peachy Dixon is a Baltimore encyclopedia. For 40 years she's waited on customers at Sabatino's. Some of her customers are pretty famous people.

"I've been at Sabatino's nearly 40 years. I've waited on Frank Sinatra, Al Pacino, Stevie Wonder, Bill Murray, among others. The restaurant used to be open every night until 3 in the morning. So when the stars came to town this was the only place they could get a decent meal after the performance," said Leonora "Peachy" Dixon.

A priest gave her the nickname "Peachy" when she was seven.

The Baltimore Bookies is her first fiction novel. She is the author of 3 autobiographies:

A Peachy Life

A Peachy Business

My Peachy City

available for purchase by contacting Peachy at
PeachyDixon1@gmail.com

'Peachy' Dixon shares stories from "Peachy and Boh's Place"

Highlandtown native shares personal story at Havre de Grace Library

By BRAD KRONER
bkroner@chespub.com

Leonora 'Peachy' DiPietro Dixon,
... waitress from Bal-

KENNETH K. LAM/BALTIMORE SUN PHOTOS

PHOTO BY BRAD KRONER

...nora 'Peachy' Dixon remarked that her book ... native.

'Peachy' puts it all on the record

Waitress recalls Unitas, Sinatra, single motherhood

By Mary Gail Hare
THE BALTIMORE SUN

A revolving rooftop restaurant in downtown Baltimore introduced Leonora DiPietro to waitressing more than 45 years ago. The stations, where staff picked up drinks and entrees, rotated constantly, too, which was too much for the new employee. She had locked herself in a linen closet to cry in frustration when her manager found her and spent the rest of the evening schooling her in the trade that would become her career.

Over the decades, she has served celebrities, politicians, sports figures and next-door neighbors, all of whom know her as Peachy, the nickname the parish priest gave a bubbly little girl with rosy cheeks.

She was born in 1941 and grew up in Highlandtown, where she still lives. She added Dixon to her name about 20 years later and kept it, though her marriage failed. For most of her nearly 70 years, she has answered to Peachy.

She started at the Circle One Rooftop Restaurant and then the Golden Arm and Haussner's, all of which are now closed. For the ... she ... worked the evening shift at Sa... ly, sometimes until 3 a.m. and ... Pacino, Will Smith, Harriso ... and Frank Sinatra.

"Sinatra really had the mo... she said. "And he was so ni... body. He came in every time ...

She recently released "A P... of life in the modest brick ro... ents raised their four childr... the house but the echoes of t... through walls decorated w... has written about raising t... living on waitress tips.

"The restaurants, that's ... said of the book, published ... family, that's the loving par...

Phil Culotta, general m... more than 30 years, descri... with long hours but rewa... have many regular and lo... third and fourth generatio... served, he said.

Dixon writes of her fat... borer, who came home d...

from the furnaces and handed roses in the backyard so tirelessly that they still bloom today. She recalls working at the Golden Arm for Johnny Unitas, the renowned Baltimore Colts quarterback who didn't balk at doing routine housekeeping himself.

"On opening night at the restaurant, there was Johnny Unitas with a plunger, headed to unclog the pipes in the ladies' room," she said.

Her uncle, Dominic (Mim!) DiPietro, was an outspoken and colorful city councilman whose constituents relied on him for just about everything. "He once made sure a blizzard didn't stop a wedding at Our Lady of Pompei," she said.

And she writes of how she took the unprecedented step, for a woman in her era, of leaving an unhappy marriage.

"The only good thing that came out of that marriage is my two children," she said.

When a knee operation sidelined Dixon, she started to write about "all the people who have touched my life." Dixon filled the pages with details of holiday celebrations. Christmas feasting started on Dec. 15, her younger brother's birthday, and the DiPeitros always hosted the neighborhood New ... ... imbedded in some of her mother's ...

WEDNESDAY, AUGUST 1, 2012

THE BALTIMORE GUI...

Little Italy waitress pens successful autobiography, starts book tv...

BY ERIK ZYGMONT
EDITOR@BALTIMOREGUIDE.COM

Waitress, author, former restaurateur, and Highlandtown native Leonora "Peachy" Dixon knows the importance of friends and family.

"You are going to make a very important decision, and your friends are going to help you out," read the 1970 horoscope that convinced her to go to Superbowl V, in which the Baltimore Colts defeated the Dallas Cowboys, thanks to Jim O'Brien's field goal in the final seconds of the game.

Peachy borrowed $138 from about 138 friends, and made the trip to Miami with her cousin and childhood friend, Clara Yuna.

The entire escapade, in which Peachy and Clara also managed to finagle a ride to the stadium on a lavish, booze-filled bus, is told in detail in her first book, A Peachy Life: Waiting on Tables and Beating the Odds in the '60s—An Italian American Woman's Story.

In April 2011, her friends helped out again, 400 of them in fact, when she held her first official signing for the book at her former employer's Sabatino's restaurant in Little Italy.

"You couldn't get in to Little Italy," laughs Peachy. "There was a traffic jam."

Maybe it was her positive outlook that pulled in the people around her to form that network of friendship and good will. It was clearly that same glowing personality that led Father Petti of Our Lady of Pompei Church to first call her "Peachy" back in her childhood.

"He came up to me and said (heavy italian accent) 'You gotta peachy cheeks!'" Peachy said. "When my family heard it, that was it."

The nickname and attitude stuck, and that same sweet optimism helped her become an author. Coming off of knee surgery a few ... ... years ago, she spent the downtime putting ... memories of her eventful life on paper.

That project grew into A Peachy Life, with about 3,500 copies sold up to now.

A Peachy Life chronicles Peachy's childhood in Highlandtown, her formative years, and her monumental decision to take her two children and leave her abusive and

addicted husband. She supported her family by waitressing at some of the city's landmark restaurants—Sabatino's, Haussner's of Highlandtown, and Johnny Unitas' Golden Arm. She met celebrities—Al Pacino for one. She got to know Unitas.

Leonora "Peachy" Dixon is a self-described "little old lady from Highlandtown." Her first book, A Peachy Life, has sold 3,500 copies.

Through it all, Peachy has had so... positive things to say about her fa... friends.

"I had a wonderful, wonderful life," she says. "To this day, I do... how my father did it, raising four ch... one salary and taking such wonde... of us."

After getting her memories on p... putting them in narrative form, P... out to have her book published. S... strategic approach.

"I only picked agents in New ... says, "because, they say, if you ma... you make it anywhere."

Peachy says that she sent mate... 20 different publishing agents, an... 20 rejection letters.

"I got put down many times," ... In 2009, however, Peachy wa... by homely singer Susan Boy... prised everybody with her p... mance of "I Dreamed a Dre... aired on Britain's Got Talent... heartfelt praise from the notor... Simon Cowell.

"I said, 'Baby, if you can ... going to do it,'" says Peachy.

CONTINUE...

Peachy: Dixon now working on second book

CONTINUED FROM PAGE...

The Beacon

FREE

IN FOCUS FOR PEOPLE OVER 50

VOL.27, NO.2   MORE than 125,000 readers throughout Greater Baltimore

Beloved waitress writes fiction

By Diane Carliner

Everyone in Baltimore, it seems, knows Peachy.

Leonora "Peachy" DePietro Dixon has waited tables at Sabatino's restaurant in Little Italy since 1974. (She received her childhood nickname for her peaches-and-cream complexion.)

With a wide circle of friends from all over Baltimore and celebrity acquaintances, she is well known for her warm-heartedness.

Among the famous people she rubbed shoulders with at Sabatino's and other local restaurants are Frank Sinatra, Cardinal Keeler, Ted Kennedy, Mother Teresa, President Jimmy Carter, Johnny Depp, Debbie Reynolds and Mohammad Ali.

A few years ago, Dixon, now in her 70s, discovered another talent in addition to being a people person: writing.

"I always thought about writing, but my parents never pushed me. My brothers have college degrees, but as a girl I was expected to get a job after high school," she recalled.

Her writing career came about as a result of an accident. A pickup truck swerved into her, injuring her knee. Spending long hours on her feet as a waitress slowed her recovery. But during that time, in part reached out to her and revealed some family stories.

With the stories, Dixon said, "Memories started flowing out of me. [My] sister came to read what I wrote. We both started to cry. 'Peachy, you have something here. Don't stop writing,' my sister said."

A lucky break

Finding an editor for her first book was a great struggle. But she was helped along the way by a Sabatino's customer who was an editor, and by Michael Olesker, a former Baltimore Sun columnist. CityLit Press published *A Peachy Life* in 2011.

As the title suggests, the book is autobiographical. It deals with her early years growing up in Highlandtown, her family life, and her strict Catholic upbringing with a father who worked at Bethlehem Steel.

These vignettes are followed by her rape on a blind date, her subsequent pregnancy and then clandestine meetings in the state, which was an abortion facility.

But she also writes about her first non-marital daughter and consummates her relationship.

Leonora "Peachy" Dixon, 72, has long been a highly popular waitress at Sabatino's in Little Italy, where she has worked since the 1970s. But she is also a published author. Her fourth book, a novel set in Baltimore, will be released in March.

"Peachy is a good storyteller, and she has the kind of life that deserves to be in a book," said Gregg Wilhelm, publisher of CityLit Press. "She and I worked really hard together crafting that manuscript, but it's all Peachy."

The book launch, held at Sabatino's, was "one of the highlights of my publishing career," Wilhelm said. The line outside the restaurant stretched around the block, he remembered.

"All the celebrities who have ever been through Sabatino's — the news reporters, the athletes — everybody showed up," Wilhelm said. "She was in her glory."

At Peachy's request, Wilhelm said he "ordered what I thought was at home amount of books for one event — and darn if we didn't sell all but two."

First book led to three more

The second book, *A Peachy Business*, published in 2016, is about her short stint in the restaurant industry and the many challenges involved in being a female restaurant owner in the 1980s and 90s.

Two years later, she published her third book, *My Peachy City*, about authentic Baltimore. Descriptions of significant local people past and present — such as former Governor William Donald Schaefer, Congresswoman Helen Bentley, Senator Barbara Mikulski

see WAITRESS, page 27

and their accomplishments — add a touch of nostalgia.

Dixon's personal experiences with the Orioles, the Ravens, Patterson Park, Haussner's, and H & S Bakery resonated with Baltimoreans.

A stab at fiction

Dixon's fourth book and most recent endeavor, *The Baltimore Bookie*, is her first attempt at fiction. In the book, the Little Italy bookies and Highlandtown bookies are in competition with each other for customers.

Drugs are involved, especially fentanyl. A woman is beaten up in a schoolyard in Highlandtown, and a mutilated dead body is found near the Department of Motor Vehicles in Glen Burnie.

High drama transpires in well-known places, such as the Inner Harbor and The Horse You Came in On bar in Fells Point. Descriptions of the Italian, Polish, Irish and German immigrants who settled the area add interest and authenticity to the tale.

The book is expected to be available at Sabatino's in March.

Family ties and local admirers

Dixon's daughter Anna Maria Carpenter, a former schoolteacher and currently a benefits manager for Calvert County, is proud of her mother's strength.

"She is in her late 70s, still very strong and still working. She is sharp, witty and funny, and loves the people she serves," she said. "Her life was a struggle, and she came through it all."

Longtime friend Reverend Robert Albright first became aware of Dixon in the early 1990s, when he saw her in a television advertisement.

"I was surprised to see a hometown girl promoting the Orioles," said Albright, a retired Catholic priest. "It reminded me of my own working-class background growing up in Pittsburgh in an area known as the slums."

At the time, Albright was a professor of religious studies at Towson University. He took some of his students to Sabatino's to meet the waitress, and the two became friends.

Although officially retired as university chaplain, he is currently an instructor with the Osher Institute, also at Towson University.

Albright has read all of Dixon's books, of course. "Her first three books are extremely authentic because of her experiences and involvement in their subjects. Peachy exposes Baltimore and its history.

"She is a marvelous example for retired people," he added, working part-time in her late 70s and writing books. The older she gets, he said, "the more exciting life is for her."

Her daughter, however, focuses on her mother's wide popularity and big heart. "People love my mother. It's a huge blessing to have people admire her and hold her so dear. They always ask for her at Sabatino's."

Dixon's books are available at Sabatino's, 901 East Fawn St., Baltimore. For more information, call the restaurant at (410) 727-2667.